Rave

OLGA BROUMAS

POEMS 1975–1999

OLGA
BROUMAS

COPPER CANYON PRESS

Deep gratitude for life and art to Jane Miller, T Begley,
Kate Carter, Sam Hamill, the Brandeis community,
Cape Cod, the Pond Village Zendo, my clients,
my sister, and to Christine Hart.

The publication of this book was supported by grants
from the Lannan Foundation, the National Endowment
for the Arts, and the Washington State Arts Commission.
Additional support was received from Elliott Bay Book
Company, Cynthia Hartwig, and the many members
who joined the Friends of Copper Canyon Press
campaign. Copper Canyon Press is in residence with
Centrum at Fort Worden State Park.

LIBRARY OF CONGRESS
CATALOGING-IN-PUBLICATION DATA

Broumas, Olga, 1949–
Rave: poems, 1975–1999 / by Olga Broumas
p. cm.
ISBN 1-55659-127-6 (alk. paper)
ISBN 1-55659-126-8 (pbk.: alk. paper)
1. Mythology, Greek Poetry. 2. Feminism Poetry.
3. Lesbians Poetry. 4. Women Poetry. 1. Title.
PS3552.R6819 A6 1999
811'.54 – DC21
99-6370
CIP

3 5 7 9 8 6 4 2
FIRST PRINTING

COPPER CANYON PRESS
Post Office Box 271
Port Townsend, Washington 98368
www.ccpress.org

CONTENTS

from

Black Holes, Black Stockings *193*

Moon

203

Perpetua *209*

PART I

CONTENTS

ix

CONTENTS

xi

.

for my mother and father

Poetry begins where death is robbed of the last word.

ODYSSEAS ELYTIS

This must be what I wanted to be doing,
Walking at night between the two deserts,
Singing.

W.S. MERWIN

Rave

OLGA BROUMAS

Caritas

Thank someone for being
that one. Walk with her
to the center of a place
and back again
singing a little song.
Burn something.

SENECA TRIBE OF
NATIVE AMERICANS

I

Erik Satie, accused
once of formlessness, composed
a sonata titled: Composition in the Form
of a Pear. When I tell you
that it would take
more brilliance than Mozart
more melancholy precision than Brahms
to compose a sonata in the form of
your breasts, you
don't believe me. I lie
next to your infidel sleep, all night
in pain
and lonely with my silenced
pleasure. Your breasts
in their moonlit pallor
invade me, lightly, like minor
fugues. I lie
between your sappling thighs, tongue
flat on your double lips, giving
voice, giving
voice. Opulent
as a continent in the rising light, you sleep

on, indifferent
to my gushing praises. It is
as it should be. Atlantis,
Cyprus, Crete, the encircled
civilizations, serene
in their tidal basins, dolphin-
loved, didn't heed to the faint, the
riotous
praise
of the lapping sea.

2

Your knees, those pinnacles
competing with the finest
dimpled, five-
year-old chins are
dancing. Ecstatic as nuns
in their delirious habit, like
runaway needles on a multiple graph,
the first organic model of
seismographs, charting
the crest I keep you on
and on till all
the sensitive numbers on the
Richter scale ring out at
once, but
silently: a choir
of sundial alarums. You reach that place,
levitated by pleasure, the first
glimpse the melting
glacier must
have had, rounding the precipice,

of what came to be known as
Niagara Falls. After all this time,
every time,
like a finger inside
the tight-gummed,
spittle-bright, atavistic
suckle of
a newborn's fragile-lipped
mouth, I
embrace you, my heart
a four-celled embryo, swimming
a pulse, a bloodstream that becomes, month
to month, less
of a stranger's, more
intimate, her
own.

3

> *There are people who do not explore the in-*
> *Sides of flowers...*
>
> SANDRA HOCHMAN

With the clear
plastic speculum, transparent
and, when inserted, pink like the convex
carapace of a prawn, flashlight in hand, I
guide you
inside the small
cathedral of my cunt. The unexpected
light dazzles you. This flesh, my darling, always
invisible like the wet
side of stones, the hidden

hemisphere of the moon, startles you
with its brilliance, the little
dome a spitting
miniature of the Haghia Sophia
with its circlet of openings
to the Mediterranean sun.
A woman-made language would
have as many synonyms for pink / light-filled / holy as
the Eskimo does
for snow. Speechless, you
shift the flashlight from
hand to hand, flickering. An orgy
of candles. Lourdes in mid-August. A flurry of
audible breaths, a seething
of holiness, and
behold
a tear
forms in the single eye, carmine
and catholic. You too, my darling, are
folded, clean
round a light-filled temple, complete
with miraculous icon, shedding
her perfect tears, in touch
with the hidden hemispheres,
the dome
of our cyclops moon.

4

She's white and her shoulders sing
like a singular vein of marble
alive and kicking in the jagged hill.
Her eyes are wet heaps

of seaweed in the sullen dusk.
Eyes of shadow and latitudes. Eyes of slate,
eyes of flint, eyes the color of certain stones
prized above all by Georgia
O'Keeffe. Eyes of an agile
wilderness, wings of a desert
moth. Her handsome hands. Each
one a duchess in her splendid gardens, each
one a pastry cook at her pliable dough, each one
a midwife at her palpable labor, the referee
of our relay race.
Her belly lulls me like an immense coastline
of dunes beneath a floating gull.
Her belly lulls me in a lustrous bowl
so precious
all the Asiatic dynasties
roll in their gilded graves, tarnished
with envy. Skin like the awning of
a ceremonial tent, the cloth draped over
the bread and wine of
an ungodly marriage. Is not this love
also a tavern? Is this meal not also
a public meal? I am encircled like a pit
in the fruit's ripe stomach, an ovum in cilia-lined
amniotic space, a drunken satellite, home
at last from its dizzy orbit.
Strike
up the music, my
love will dance. The loaf
of bread held against her breasts, the blade
in her nimble fingers, her feet stamping patterns
like snakes in the circle of dust, her waist a

scorpion's, she'll
dance, dance
the bread dance, slicing
out flawless ovals from
her inexhaustible loaf.

5

Imagine
something so beautiful
your liver would swell with contraband
chemicals, laughter, the dangerous
and infectious song.
Something so fine
you'd need no alibi for
your avid enchantment. A small
thing to start with: a special hairline
on a special nape, bent
low towards you. Imagine now
how your fingertips throb. You follow
the spinal valley, dipping
its hollow core like a ladle of light
in your ministering fingers.
Intuit the face
like that of a woman's
inscribed upon the porous
tablets of the law, rich with an age,
with tenderness, various, and like a map
of recurring lives. Here the remnants of
an indefatigable anger, the jubilant
birth-yell, here the indelible
covens of pleasure, a web
of murmurs, a lace

mantilla of sighs.
Recapture
the fleshy mouth full of fissures, the tongue
on the sated lip, the residual flare
of a regal nostril, the purple shade
of an earlobe, the eyebrows meeting
squarely above the lids.
You laugh
at this like a daughter, a young
sprig of amaranth caught
in your gelding teeth, that fade-
less flower you call a pigweed, a prince's
feather, a love-
lies-bleeding. But
not this love. Laugh, lover, laugh
with me. In that side-
splitting reservoir, in the promised calm
of its heaving waters, you'll
bend, you'll see this woman's
beautiful
and familiar face.

Beginning
with O

Sometimes, as a child

when the Greek sea
was exceptionally calm,
the sun not so much a pinnacle
as a perspiration of light, your brow and the sky
meeting on the horizon, sometimes

you'd dive
from the float, the pier, the stone
promontory, through water so startled
it held the shape of your plunge, and there

in the arrested heat of the afternoon
without thought, effortless
as a mantra turning
you'd turn
in the paused wake of your dive, enter
the suck of the parted waters, you'd emerge

clean caesarean, flinging
live rivulets from your hair, your own
breath arrested. Something immaculate, a chance

crucial junction: time, light, water
had occurred, you could feel your bones
glisten
translucent as mermaids' spines.
                              In rain-
green Oregon now, approaching thirty, sometimes

the same
rare concert of light and spine
resonates in my bones, as glistening
starfish, lover, your fingers
beach up.

TWELVE ASPECTS
OF GOD

for Sandra McKee

Leda and Her Swan

You have red toenails, chestnut
hair on your calves, oh let
me love you, the fathers
are lingering in the background
nodding assent.

I dream of you
shedding calico from
slow-motion breasts, I dream
of you leaving with
skinny women, I dream you know.

The fathers are nodding like
overdosed lechers, the fathers approve
with authority: Persian emperors, ordering
that the sun shall rise
every dawn, set
each dusk. I dream.

White bathroom surfaces
rounded basins you
stand among
loosening
hair, arms, my senses.

The fathers are Dresden figurines
vestigial, anecdotal
small sculptures shaped
by the hands of nuns. Yours

crimson-tipped, take no part in that
crude abnegation. Scarlet

liturgies shake our room, amaryllis blooms
in your upper thighs, water lily
on mine, fervent delta

the bed afloat, sheer
linen billowing
on the wind: Nile, Amazon, Mississippi.

Amazon Twins

I

You wanted to compare, and there
we were, eyes on each eye, the lower
lids
squinting
suddenly awake

though the light was dim. Looking away
some time ago, you'd said
    the eyes are live
    animals, domiciled in our head
but more than the head

is crustacean-like. Marine
eyes, marine
odors. Everything live
(tongue, clitoris, lip and lip)
swells in its moist shell. I remember the light

warped round our bodies finally
crustal, striated with sweat.

II

In the gazebo-like café, you gave
me food from your plate, alert
to my blood-sweet hungers
double-edged
in the glare of the sun's
and our own
twin heat. Yes, there
we were, breasts on each side, Amazons
adolescent at twenty-nine

privileged
to keep the bulbs and to feel the blade
swell, breath-sharp
on either side. In that public place

in that public place.

Triple Muse

I

Three of us sat
in the early summer, our instruments
cared for, our bodies dark

and one stirred the stones on
the earthen platter, till the salt
veins aligned, and she read the cast:

Whatever is past
and has come to an end
cannot be brought back by sorrow

II

False things
we've made seem true, by charm, by music. Faked
any trick when it pleased us

and laughed, faked
too when it didn't. The audience couldn't tell, invoking
us absently, stroking their fragile beards, waiting

for inspiration
served up like dinner, or sex. Past. Here
each of us knows, herself, the mineral-bright path.

III

It's been said, we are of one mind.
It's been said, she is happy whom
we, of the muses, love.

Spiral Mountain: the cabin
full of our tools: guitar, tape deck, video
every night

stars we can cast the dice by. We are
of one mind, tuning
our instruments to ourselves, by our triple light.

Io

One would know nothing.
One would begin by the touch
return to her body,
one would forget
even the three
soft cages
where summer lasts.

One would regret nothing.
One would first touch the mouth
then the warm
pulsing places that wait
that wait
and the last song around them
a shred of light.

A crumpled apron, a headcloth, a veil.
One would keep nothing.

By the still mouths of fear
one would listen. Desire
would spill past each lip
and caution. That which is light
would remain.

That which is
still would grow fertile.

Thetis

No. I'm not tired, the tide
is late tonight, go
with your sisters, go
sleep, go play.
           No? Then come
closer, sit here, look

where we strung the fruit, hammocks of
apples, dates, orange peel. Look
at the moon
lolling between them, indolent
as a suckled breast. Do you understand

child, how the moon, the tide
is our own
image? Inland
the women call themselves Tidal Pools
call their water jars Women, insert
sponge and seaweed
under each curly, triangular thatch. Well

there's the salt lip, finally
drawing back. You must understand
everything that caresses you

will not be like this
moon-bright water, pleasurable, fertile
only with mollusks and fish. There are still
other fluids, fecund, tail-whipped
with seed. There are ways
to evade them. Go
get a strand

of kelp. Fold it, down in your palm
like a cup, a hood. Good.
Squat down beside me.
Facing the moon.

Dactyls

THE PALM

Her furrowed heart, her brittle life, her mind
dissected by fate. Are these adjectives permanent?
She frowns
at her open hand.

LINE OF THE HEART

Up the long hill, the earth rut steamed in the strange sun.
We, walking between its labia, loverlike, palm to palm.

LINE OF THE MIND

The branch splits in two: I will eat both the male
and the female fruit. Gnaw back the fork to its simple crotch.

LIFE LINE

Metropolis: Mother
city. Whose columns, bulging
vertically like braced thighs, endure
the centuries, and the brittle light.

THE FATE

By the left lintel, lavender. Through the left
lobe, twin cymbals. Who dares stop hungry
Fate from her salad, her crazy
leveling meal.

Circe

THE CHARM

The fire bites, the fire bites. Bites
to the little death. Bites

till she comes to nothing. Bites
on her own sweet tongue. She goes on. Biting.

THE ANTICIPATION

They tell me a woman waits, motionless
till she's wooed. I wait

spiderlike, effortless as they weave
even my web for me, tying the cord in knots

with their courting hands. Such power
over them. And the spell

their own. Who could release them? Who
would untie the cord

with a cloven hoof?

THE BITE

What I wear in the morning pleases
me: green shirt, skirt of wine. I am wrapped

in myself as the smell of night
wraps round my sleep when I sleep

outside. By the time
I get to the corner

bar, corner store, corner construction
site, I become divine. I turn

men into swine. Leave
them behind me whistling, grunting, wild.

Maenad

Hell has no fury like women's fury. Scorned
in their life by the living
sons they themselves
have set loose, like a great gasp
through a fleshy nostril.
Hell has no fury.

Hell has no fury like fury of women. Scorned
by their daughters who claim paternity, wed-
lock, deliverance
from the pulsing apron-strings of the apron
tied round their omphalos, that maternal
and terrible brand. Hell has no fury.

Hell has no fury like the fury of women. Scorned
from birth by their mothers who
must deliver the heritage: signs, methods,
artifacts, what-they-remember
intact to them, and who have no time
for sentiment, only warnings. Hell has no fury.

And hell has no fury like fury of women. Scorning
themselves in each other's image
they would deny that image
even to god
as she laughs at them, scornfully
through her cloven maw. Hell has no rage like this

women's rage.

Aphrodite

The one with the stone cups

and the stone face, and the grinding
stone settled
between her knees, the one with stone

in her bosom, with stones
in her kidneys, a heart of pure
stone, the one with the stony lips, the one

with the thighs of marble, with petrified
genitals, the one whose glance
turns to stone

this idol, stones
through her ears, stones round her neck, her
wrists, round her fingers, a stone

in her navel, stones in her shoes, this
woman so like a stone
statue, herself

a stone, stands
in the stone square, midway
between the stone-high steeple, the stone-

round well, a stone
in her stone-still hand, and a stony will
waiting

for what will land, stiff
as a long stone, on the grinding
stone, on

her lap.

Calypso

I've gathered the women like talismans, one
by one. They first came for tarot card
gossip, mystified
by my hands, by offers
cut with escape. They came

undone in my studio, sailing long eyes, heavy
with smoke and wet
with the force of dream: a vagina
folding mandala-like
out of herself, in full bloom. I used them. I used

the significance
of each card to uphold the dream, soon
they came back with others. I let the bitch
twitch in my lap. I listened. I let the tea steep
till the pot was black. Soon

there was no need for cards. We would use
stills from our daily lives, every woman
a constellation of images, every
portrait each other's chart.
We came together

like months
in a lunar year, measured in nights, dividing
perfectly into female phases. Like women anywhere
living in groups we had synchronous menses. And had
no need of a wound, a puncture, to seal our bond.

Demeter

I

Dependence... the male
poet said, *that touchstone
of happiness.* Dependence
on what, happiness
for which one of us, child, segment
of skin and cartilage you have
claimed, and I, yes
have allowed you.
                    Do
close the shutters, the drawers, the cupboard
doors. They remind
me of open graves – will you die before me, my
bundle of flesh?

II

What does one say to a child?

What does one say to the little fingers, sticky
with libido, reaching
compulsively out of the dark
enclosure to face
the light?
            All noble resins:
frankincense, amber, tears of a mother grieving
a mortal child.
                    Anne. Sylvia. Virginia.
Adrienne the last, magnificent last.

III

Let there be light, let there be light.
                              The terror
of newborns, sliding
down on its medical and
convenient glare.
                    Even your sleep in
a darkened room, and the room itself, shuttered
around you, are analogues
of that place you were shocked from: cold
breath, sharp sight.
                        You refuse sleep.
Rage at the night. All your life
will you cringe from the dark, bake
your skin in the open sun, hate my gut
that betrayed you? Child,
                          even here,
in his own book, it says
who held the spotlight
as you delivered yourself, screaming
into its gleaming, mechanical eye.

Artemis

Let's not have tea. White wine
eases the mind along
the slopes
of the faithful body, helps

any memory once engraved
on the twin
chromosome ribbons, emerge, tentative
from the archaeology of an excised past.

I am a woman
who understands
the necessity of an impulse whose goal or origin
still lie beyond me. I keep the goat

for more
than the pastoral reasons. I work
in silver the tongue-like forms
that curve round a throat

an armpit, the upper
thigh, whose significance stirs in me
like a curviform alphabet
that defies

decoding, appears
to consist of vowels, beginning with O, the O-
mega, horseshoe, the cave of sound.
What tiny fragments

survive, mangled into our language.
I am a woman committed to
a politics
of transliteration, the methodology

of a mind
stunned at the suddenly
possible shifts of meaning – for which
like amnesiacs

in a ward on fire, we must
find words
or burn.

THE KNIFE AND
THE BREAD

for Stephen

betrothal / the bride's lament

when all this is over we'll find ourselves
in a big room with wooden floors walls & ceilings
a stone hedge outside & the dogs
barking hard at the threshold

even now we are building this room
we make the roof high stud the crossbeams with hooks
we keep two large trunks rough till the end &
use them for posts here & here now
look how they make the room
strong we say & the splintered bark throws its mouths wide in
laughter & anguish we dare not claim

we'll find ourselves in a shrubbed
acrid land
            the rough logs have worn
from the rub & saltwater sheathing them year after year
the leather cords have turned dark
stained & pliant & we've found some names
for the laughter of vanished bark
names our skin calls

for we have yielded by now
to the clasping of nights on this island
where we gyrate like landed squid
immigrants left by even this awkward
most rudimentary language we use
to signify thankfulness appreciation & pain

we will be stranded my love
as lone & exiled as we have never dared hope
& this word will be lost to us too: hope

or will be there like dreams of rain
rushing forests spring rivers like dreams of dreams

we'll grow to crave shadow
to dress our fair limbs with dust

any memory of pale pastel sheets
smooth & ironed & turned down to wait the sliding
of thigh against thigh & the pearly residue of it all
will be there only to taunt us & even then
we will not know the best of it

but will lie on the coarse sand still in the waning moons
& believe that the flapping of wavelets
is maybe the old promise
again in the night come to comfort us
song comfort promise believe will be the new
curses we must atone for

though we'll have song my love
we'll hear the scryings of cleft-winged birds
dashed time & over against the rock
& pick our beat from their gasping hearts
pulsing a minor flood on our lips
here & here

            yes song & faith too
the old bag of needles might be there
listening & her senile cronies calm peace & solace but
who love who could grant absolution from this
raging clarity its relentless fear &
even if would you want to

gentle rags garnered weeds bitter ashes the days
still pass
            we forget the hammer the cold slate shakes
in morning light we repeat the grief
break the milk's skin
sink what sorrow persists in its creamy torpor
call it dream gone

outside the garden throws hasty vines down the gravel path
& the structure
a half-built & peak-roofed cell
wears the dew's sparkling mail like a sneer

we rise together our bodies blind in venetian light
fat like the birds in our fish-tank windows
& smooth where the sweat still lasts
                                    or semen
smooth with the loose pride of now when it's all
over love pride will be first to go
& we stretch our limbs from some odd stiffness
pull on our downy sheaths

when the latch slips its lock this time
past our linked fingers
more doors than this
one are closing

plunging into the improbable

we are partners in this bee
partners
& spell each other against the wall of fame

you will know what i mean, words
are supposed to claw you with
beauty, tear at you
spirant by sonorant
tongue by tongue

some weird mutation of orgasm
a spasm

the film develops in its aluminum skull
life goes on with its glee
love its passion
equally

you or i
trade off words, partners
suddenly & at random: like
lights in the high-rise windows, a flick
of a tongue now
a hiss

we had signed with the brush of thighs
held back all clappers
but one, & that

one pealing
odors of covered sprouts
yeast & shellfish, odors of fluid, the dark-
room dark & the metal bone

what night could wish for more equal meal?

more suitable silver?

others stalk lovers, the wild
fuck

in this room
the slice of skin that reveals me
to you
is as meaningful, later
sleep carves our body out of a log
we wake up falling

the stage dismantled, pedestal gone
the audience even
dancing to instrumentals

a wooden ladle
twists in our mouth for the alphabet
but the tongue is no soup bone
the teeth give no broth

the film has developed
prolific in chemical baths: breasts
curving sharply to wrinkled mounds
the glans like an unshelled cervix
the cunt-folds sweating
the ass-hole sweet

here we are, a curve
on a piece of paper, a line of ink
the improbable in high contrast, a contact
sheet, black & white

here we are, fixed
in eidetic memory, film
of the greedy mind, tapedecks & journals, each
other's voice in deep sleep played
back every morning

flesh-toned
the celluloid unfurls
round the cogs with a whisper, the stars
are silent, the sky
exposed

Love Lines

*for those islands in the Aegean
whose harbors are too small for
commercial lines*

our muffled phone & the through-
town train, tonight i
fuse them
in sleep as their rumble
fades, rhythmically, & another's
sound echoes, a ship's

stack, hooting
desultorily past
small-hulled islands, each port a knothole
lapped shut

the water is tender, green, curls
softly innocent, a lazy noose in the sunlight
i loved you, i know

now, water swells
wood, lungs, i loved you, i go

past shallows to
sashaying algae to
prowling kelp, remote
inaccessible

as the harbor, no phone
or faith

love orbits
us, all night
long, your cock is an instrument
in my palm to gauge by, at breakfast you pour

the coffee, i hold
my tongue, what i keep from you
keeps
me from you, the ship

is fading, like sunlit frost, silver
gleams on our table, mugs shine
red as cranberries, blue as frostbite, i want

to hold
on, not back, brave
morning's fierce tangibility –
tell you

still, by the dry light, i grow
edgy, bristle
defenses, a pine-
cone in fire

if i were a man, or you a woman, anything
would be easier than this: one man
you, me

one woman, lost
in the shrinking summer

our breakfast done

memory piece / for Baby Jane

your touch is gentle on
your own skin, your shoulders love you
at night

your mother calls from across the country
collect, awake
from a bad dream, you are
too far away, she tells you
secrets, your free

hand gathers you
up, knee to nipple, your own
body

becomes your mother
your own lap

you spelled your name like a cabaret
B.J., five feet two inches of
tough luck, you made it

sound good – baby
three years of balancing
on a madman's pole, with
his tray, his apron
for food & tips
three years
more for tuition, six months
for love

in the bathtub you
bathe yourself, with such care
your ex-husband shivers, your breasts

shine on the water
adrift with hair

you've noticed the cat
doesn't leap to your lap in the morning, she
haunts the closets, a neutered
animal, fat
on food

you think of ends, lumescent
periods, islands
at line's term

abortion

you pull the plug & rub
creamrinse on pubic hair still
light with summer

you rinse down spirals
on crescent thighs

turning in
to herself, your body finds nothing
hard, nothing quiet, that wish
is blood, you have no wound

that would heal, you are a woman
you bleed

neither pregnant nor fallow, not
pill-controlled, you throw
mud into pots that might
hold water, the same

palm curves on
the wheel that curves round
your belly, at night
i remember, you'd
sing

to yourself

the knife & the bread

for the women of Cyprus, '74

in the morning
the room is sharp with mirrors
the light is helpless

i skirt
your live-wire laughter
i embrace the wall, fat curtains bellying
in on the wind: cooler weather

i tell you violence
perseveres, the light being cruel
itself
to the beveled edges
i look, i cannot forget
though i flap my mind like a breathless tongue

i am sick with knives, knives
slashing breasts away, handheld
knives cutting wounds to be raped
by cocks, thick blunt knives
sheathing blood, knives
paring cheeks away
knives
in the belly

apples won't comfort me
this isn't love

this dance i pant from not safe
or ancient, its steps
marred with the fall of women
falling
from cliffs, walls, anything
to escape this war
without national

boundary, this fear
beyond tribes

you, over there, dark
as a church, insular
can ignore the light
in the cruel mirrors

you laugh / a knife
in your
belly would
slice only guts

when the enemy comes
the men run to the mountains

they are rebels
they sing to their knives
wash out their hair & prepare themselves
for a manly death

young women hide in the cellars

old women wait

when the enemy comes
they make the old women dance
make them sing / underground
an infant begins to wail
in her single knowledge

the old ones sing louder
dance faster, fit these new words
to their frenzied song: *daughter, oh*
throttle her
or slaughter her
or gag her on your breast

you have seen their breasts
rolling in mounds, little pyramids
in the soldiers' wake

i slice the bread
in the kitchen, i hold the knife

steady against the grain
that feeds us
all
indiscriminate
as an act of god

i hold the knife
& i slice the bread / the west
light low on the blade
liquid, exhausted
the food

chaste on the table & powerless
to contain us, how long
can i keep the knife

in its place

INNOCENCE

for Claire, my mother

Innocence

... *the sound of one hand clapping*

I

Manita's the Queen. Love and Love
lying by her, one
on each side. I
am the Jester, the
smallest one, I roll
round the bed at Manita's feet, the floor
tangled with cast-off garments. I flick my sharp
tongue at Love. I adore
Manita
the Queen
at the foot of the bed, each hand so deep
in Loves' collapsible caves. Manita kneeling
in the midst of Love.
Manita talking
with God.

II

Manita talking with God. God
appears

among us, elusive, the extra
hand none of us – Love, Love, Jester, Queen –
can quite locate, fix, or escape. Extra
hand, extra
pleasure. A hand
with the glide of a tongue, a hand
precise as an eyelid, a hand with a sense
of smell, a hand that will dance
to its liquid moan.
God's hand

loose on the four of us like a wind
on the grassy hills of the South.

III

I take my Love to Manita. Swift-boned, green-
eyed, dressed in her dark skin and hair, I take my Love in
on fire. Manita moans.
Manita's hands

flow
delicate as insects, agile
as fish, cool as the shifting water, the night-
quiet lake. I take my Love to her hands on
fire. She takes my Love.

IV

She takes my Love to her passions, sweet
bruises on her dark skin, her nipples
sucked up like pears, the small
hand of God
inventing
itself again, wind
on Manita's hair. Neither

Love moves. Queen and the Jester the
merging shadows on wall and ceiling, the candle thick
as a young tree, bright
with green fire.
Manita's Love

opens herself to me, my sharp
Jester's tongue, my
cartwheels of pleasure. The Queen's own pearl
at my fingertips, and Manita pealing

my Jester's bells on our four
small steeples, as Sunday dawns
clear in February, and God claps and claps
her one hand.

Four Beginnings / for Kyra

1

You raise
your face from mine, parting
my breath like water, hair falling
away in its own wind, and your eyes –
green in the light like honey – surfacing
on my body, awed
with desire, speechless, this common dream.

2

You bore your marriage like a misconceived
animal, and have the scars, the pale
ridged tissue round front and back
for proof. For proof. Tonight

we cross into each other's language. I take your hand
hesitant still with regret
into that milky landscape, where braille
is a tongue for lovers, where tongue,
fingers, lips
share a lidless eye.

3

I was surprised myself – the image of the lithe
hermaphroditic lover a staple of
every fantasy, bought, borrowed, or mine. We never did
mention the word, unqualified: I love:
your hair, I love: your feet, toes, tender nibbles, I love:

I love. You are the memory
of each desire that ran, dead-end, into a mind
programmed to misconstrue it. A mind inventing

neurosis, anxiety, phobia, a mind expertly camouflaged
from the thought of love
for a woman, its native
love.

4
I in my narrow body, spellbound
against your flesh.

Song / for Sanna

*... in this way the future enters
into us, in order to transform itself
in us before it happens.*
RILKE

What hasn't happened
intrudes, so much
hasn't yet happened. In the steamy

kitchens we meet in, kettles
are always boiling, water for tea, the steep
infusions we occupy
hands and mouth with, steam
filming our breath, a convenient

subterfuge, a disguise
for the now
sharp intake, the measured
outlet of air, the sigh, the gutting
loneliness

of the present where
what hasn't happened will
not be ignored, intrudes, separates
from the conversation like milk
from cream, desire

rising between the cups, brimming
over our saucers, clouding the minty
air, its own
aroma a pungent
stress, once again, you will get
up, put on your coat, go

home to the safer passions, moisture
clinging still to your spoon, as the afternoon
wears on, and I miss, I
miss you.

Lullaby

I see you, centered
along the long
axis of the house, as I come in

to your wide perspective
that endless corridor, the light
drawling forever on the lip of darkness, your long
skin radiant, its stubborn resistance
to summer tan. I see you

signaling like a white flag
in the square of your mother's crocheted
and labyrinth quilt. Brown,

black, amber, white, and that treacherous
red like a border around
the luminous hull
of your body. You leaned

into me like a ship embracing
the waters it was meant to shun, the dangerous
undertow it was meant to float on
and not claim. My love

this love has not been
forbidden. Its one risk: sailing
down through the warm laterals of the heart
to a windless bay. One of our mothers prays for this song

to survive
her own deafened ears, the other
pieces together a second quilt, one that will

cover us, neither for shame, nor
decency, but

as the chill
streetlights fluoresce on our light sleep, finally
tucking us in, for warmth.

Blues / for J.C.

Letting go, woman, is not as easy as pride
or commitment
to civilization would
have us think. Loveletters crowding against the will:

The esplanade of your belly, I said, *that*
shallow and gleaming spoon. You
said, *Not quite*
an epiphany, our bodies breathing
like greedy gills, *not quite*
an epiphany, but close, close. I loved you

then for that
willful precision, the same
precision with which you now
extricate
cool as a surgeon
your amphibian heart. My mouth,

blind in the night to pride, circles
your absence, absurd as one
fish, kissing
compulsively through the vertigo
of the deep

silence
an ocean, dimly perceived
like an aftertaste: my own salt, my fish-
bowl gyrations, my beached
up mouth.

Bitterness

She who loves roses must be patient
and not cry out when she is pierced by thorns.
SAPPHO

In parody
of a grade-B film, our private
self-conscious soapie, as we fall
into the common, suspended disbelief of love, you ask
will I still be
here tomorrow, next week, tonight you ask am I really
here. My passion delights

and surprises you, comfortable
as you've been without it. Lulled,
comfortable as a float myself in your real
and rounded arms, I can only smile
back, indulgently
at such questions. In the second reel –

a season of weeks, two
flights across the glamorous Atlantic, one
orgy and the predictable divorce
scenes later – I'm fading out
in the final close-up
alone. As one

heroine of this
two-bit production to the other, how long
did you, did we both know
the script
meant you to wake up doubting
in those first nights, not me, my daytime
serial solvency, but yours.

Beauty and the Beast

For years I fantasized pain
driving, driving
me over each threshold
I thought I had, till finally
the joy in my flesh would break
loose with the terrible
strain, and undulate
in great spasmic circles, centered
in cunt and heart. I clung to pain

because, as a drunk
and desperate boy once said, stumbling from the party
into the kitchen and the two
women there, "Pain
is the only reality." I rolled
on the linoleum with mirth, too close
to his desperation to understand, much less
to help. Years

of that reality. Pain the link
to existence: pinch your own tissue, howl
yourself from sleep. But that night was too soon
after passion
had shocked the marrow alive in my hungry bones. The boy
fled from my laughter
painfully, and I
leaned and touched, leaned
and touched you, mesmerized, woman, stunned

by the tangible
pleasure that gripped my ribs, every time
like a caged beast, bewildered
by this late, this essential heat.

Cinderella

... the joy that isn't shared
I heard, dies young.
ANNE SEXTON, 1928–1974

Apart from my sisters, estranged
from my mother, I am a woman alone
in a house of men
who secretly
call themselves princes, alone
with me usually, under cover of dark. I am the one allowed in

to the royal chambers, whose small foot conveniently
fills the slipper of glass. The woman writer, the lady
umpire, the madam chairman, anyone's wife.
I know what I know.
And I once was glad

of the chance to use it, even alone
in a strange castle, doing overtime on my own, cracking
the royal code. The princes spoke
in their fathers' language, were eager to praise me
my nimble tongue. I am a woman in a state of siege, alone

as one piece of laundry, strung on a windy clothesline a
mile long. A woman co-opted by promises: the lure
of a job, the ruse of a choice, a woman forced
to bear witness, falsely
against my kind, as each
other sister was judged inadequate, bitchy, incompetent,
jealous, too thin, too fat. I know what I know.
What sweet bread I make

for myself in this prosperous house
is dirty, what good soup I boil turns
in my mouth to mud. Give
me my ashes. A cold stove, a cinder-block pillow, wet
canvas shoes in my sisters', my sisters' hut. Or I swear

I'll die young
like those favored before me, hand-picked each one
for her joyful heart.

Rapunzel

*A woman
who loves a woman
is forever young.*
ANNE SEXTON

Climb
through my hair, climb in
to me, love

hovers here like a mother's wish.
You might have been, though you're not
my mother. You let loose like hair, like static
her stilled wish, relentless
in me and constant as
tropical growth. Every hair

on my skin curled up, my spine
an enraptured circuit, a loop of memory, your first
private touch. How many women
have yearned
for our lush perennial, found

themselves pregnant, and had
to subdue their heat, drown out their appetite
with pickles and harsh weeds. How many
grew to confuse greed
with hunger, learned to grow thin on the bitter
root, the mandrake, on their sills. *Old*

*bitch, young
darling.* May those who speak them
choke on their words, their hunger freeze

in their veins like lard.
Less innocent

in my public youth
than you, less forbearing, I'll break the hush
of our cloistered garden, our harvest continuous
as a moan, the tilled bed luminous
with the future
yield. Red

vows like tulips. Rows
upon rows of kisses from all lips.

Sleeping Beauty

I sleep, I sleep
too long, sheer hours
hound me, out
of bed and into clothes, I wake
still later, breathless, heart
racing, sleep
peeling off like a hairless
glutton, momentarily
slaked. Cold

water shocks me
back from the dream. I see
lovebites like fossils: *something
that did exist*

dreamlike, though
dreams have the perfect alibi, no
fingerprints, evidence
that a mirror could float
back in your own face, gleaming
its silver eye. Lovebites like fossils. Evidence.
Strewn

round my neck like a ceremonial
necklace, suddenly
snapped apart.

Blood. Tears. The vital
salt of our body. Each
other's mouth.
Dreamlike

the taste of you
sharpens my tongue like a thousand shells,
bitter, metallic. I know

as I sleep
that my blood runs clear
as salt
in your mouth, my eyes.

City-center, mid-
traffic, I
wake to your public kiss. Your name
is Judith, your kiss a sign

to the shocked pedestrians, gathered
beneath the light that means
stop
in our culture
where red is a warning, and men
threaten each other with final violence: *I will drink*
your blood. Your kiss
is for them

a sign of betrayal, your red
lips suspect, unspeakable
liberties as
we cross the street, kissing
against the light, singing, *This*
is the woman I woke
from sleep, the woman that woke
me sleeping.

Rumpelstiltskin

First night.
Mid-winter.
Frightened
with pleasure as I came.
Into your arms, salt
crusting the aureoles.
Our white breasts. Tears
and tears. You
saying
I don't know
if I'm hurting or loving
you. I
didn't either.
We went on
trusting. Your will to care
for me intense
as a laser. Slowly
my body's cellblocks
yielding
beneath its beam.

I have to write of these things. We were grown
women, well
traveled in our time.

Did anyone
ever encourage you, you ask
me, casual
in afternoon light. You blaze
fierce with protective anger as I shake

my head, puzzled, remembering, no
no. You blaze

a beauty you won't claim. To name
yourself beautiful makes you as vulnerable
as feeling
pleasure and claiming it
makes me. I call you lovely. Over

and over, cradling
your ugly memories as they burst
their banks, tears and tears, I call
you lovely. Your face
will come to trust that judgment, to bask
in its own clarity like sun. Grown women. Turning

heliotropes to our own, to our lovers' eyes.

Laughter. New in my lungs still, awkward
on my face. Fingernails
growing back
over decades of scar and habit, bottles
of bitter quinine rubbed into them, and chewed
on just the same. We are not the same. Two

women, laughing
in the streets, loose-limbed
with other women. Such things are dangerous.
Nine million

have burned for less.

How to describe
what we didn't know
exists: a mutant organ, its function to feel
intensely, to heal by immersion, a fluid
element, crucial
as amnion, sweet milk
in the suckling months.

Approximations.
The words we need are extinct.

Or if not extinct
badly damaged: the proud Columbia
stubbing
her bound-up feet on her dammed-
up bed. Helpless with excrement. Daily

by accident, against
what has become our will through years
of deprivation, we spawn the fluid
that cradles us, grown
as we are, and at a loss
for words. Against all currents, upstream
we spawn
in each other's blood.

Tongues
sleepwalking in caves. Pink shells. Sturdy
diggers. Archaeologists of the right
the speechless zones
of the brain.

Awake, we lie
if we try to use them, to salvage some part
of the loamy dig. It's like
forgiving each other, you said
borrowing from your childhood priest.
Sister, to wipe clean

with a musty cloth
what is clean already
is not forgiveness, the clumsy housework
of a bachelor god. We both know, well
in our prime, which is cleaner: the cave-
dwelling womb, or the colonized
midwife:

the tongue.

Little Red Riding Hood

I grow old, old
without you, Mother, landscape
of my heart. No child, no daughter between my bones
has moved, and passed
out screaming, dressed in her mantle of blood

as I did
once through your pelvic scaffold, stretching it
like a wishbone, your tenderest skin
strung on its bow and tightened
against the pain. I slipped out like an arrow, but not before

the midwife
plunged to her wrist and guided
my baffled head to its first mark. High forceps
might, in that one instant, have accomplished
what you and that good woman failed
in all these years to do: cramp
me between the temples, hobble
my baby feet. Dressed in my red hood, howling, I went—

evading
the white-clad doctor and his fancy claims: microscope,
stethoscope, scalpel, all
the better to see with, to hear,
and to eat—straight from your hollowed basket
into the midwife's skirts. I grew up

good at evading, and when you said,
"Stick to the road and forget the flowers, there's
wolves in those bushes, mind
where you got to go, mind

you get there," I
minded. I kept

to the road, kept
the hood secret, kept what it sheathed more
secret still. I opened
it only at night, and with other women
who might be walking the same road to their own
grandma's house, each with her basket of gifts, her small hood
safe in the same part. I minded well. I have no daughter

to trace that road, back to your lap with my laden
basket of love. I'm growing
old, old
without you. Mother, landscape
of my heart, architect of my body, what other gesture
can I conceive

to make with it
that would reach you, alone
in your house and waiting, across this improbable forest
peopled with wolves and our lost, flower-gathering
sisters they feed on.

Snow White

I could never want her (my mother)
until I myself had been wanted.
By a woman.
SUE SILVERMARIE

Three women
on a marriage bed, two
mothers and two daughters.
All through the war we slept
like this, grand-
mother, mother, daughter. Each night
between you, you pushed and pulled
me, willing
from warmth to warmth.

Later we fought so
bitterly through the peace
that father blanched in his uniform,
battlelined forehead milky
beneath the khaki brim.

We fought like mad-
women till the house-
hold shuddered, crockery fell, the bed-
clothes heaved in the only passion
they were, those maddening
peacetime years,
to know.

A woman
who loves a woman
who loves a woman
who loves a man.

        If the circle
be unbroken...
           Three years
into my marriage I woke with this
from an unspeakable dream
about you, fingers
electric, magnetized, repelling
my husband's flesh. Blond, clean,
miraculous, this alien
instrument I had learned to hone,
to prize, to pride myself on, instrument
for a music I couldn't dance,
cry or lose
anything to.
        A curious
music, an un-
catalogued rhyme, mother / daughter, we lay
the both of us awake
that night you straddled
two continents and the wet
opulent ocean to visit us, bringing
your gifts.
        Like two halves
of a two-colored apple – red

with discovery, green with fear – we lay
hugging the wall between us, whitewash
leaving its telltale tracks.
                              Already
some part of me had begun
the tally, dividing
the married spoils, claiming
your every gift.

Don't curse me, Mother, I couldn't bear
the bath
of your bitter spittle.
                              No salve
no ointment in a doctor's tube, no brew
in a witch's kettle, no lover's mouth, no friend
or god could heal me
if your heart
turned in anathema, grew stone
against me.
                              Defenseless
and naked as the day
I slid from you
twin voices keening and the cord
pulsing our common protest, I'm coming back
back to you
woman, flesh
of your woman's flesh, your fairest, most
faithful mirror,

my love
transversing me like a filament
wired to the noonday sun.

Receive
me, Mother.

Soie Sauvage

Oregon Landscape with Lost Lover

I take my bike
and ride down to the river
and put my feet into the water
and watch the ten toes play distortions

with the light. I had forgotten all this time
how good it is to sit by water
in sun all day and never have to leave
the river moving

as no lover ever moved
widehipped deadsure and delicate –
after a while I cannot bear
to look. Pleasure dilates me

open as a trellis
free of its green sharp glossy leaves like tongues
made out of mirrors gossiping
in the sun the wind. By which

I mean
somehow
free of the self.
Through all the hungry-eyed

criss-crossing slits along the trellis
finding them leaving them
bare and clean the widehipped delicate
green river flows

voluptuous as any lover anywhere
has been.

Five Interior Landscapes

for Stephen

I

It's all right. Things slow down. Some light
shines in the convex mirror. The candle burns.
Someone dictates a poem. The blue
field of the sheet live with wiggling
poppies, lashing their sperm-tail stems.
The special sheet, bought for the double
bed of the sleeping loft, four pillows
at its head and feet. Here
one pillow's enough. Inside the sleeping
bag, red afghan
keeps my feverish body not only warm
but dry. I'm not prepared for this. How much
I miss you.

II

The pressure falls sometimes so low
in my veins I can't breathe hard enough
to force the double
vocal cords and call. Next room a woman
friend respects my closed door. Like me
and unlike me, is silent. Right side, arm, thigh
shake for an hour in what Leah who massages me
at home calls
fear. But shaking from the central
muscle to the long thin bone, it puts
more fear in me than it lets go. Not only suffering
but that no one knows
how I suffer. I've found
thermometers are useful props

for saying no to calls from poets' parties. It lies
by the bed like a dictated song. Later I write
or try to write
from life.

III

Still they decide to have a party.
I do not recognize this life. Drinking and drinking
in noisy halls full of smoke for pleasure. The noise
finds me staring wall to wall, alone, a stranger
to my home-brought treasures. Blue
flowered sheet, red afghan, mirror
shining its scooped-out face. It's all
right. The candle burns. Epiphanies
are only numinous
clichés. Something you've known
the words to all your life undone by Nina
Simone, voice and piano. Be grateful. Stockpile.
Fastidiously, keep your body clean. Live
like a poet you'll write
like one.

IV

Baths, showers, water. The padded
well-soaped scrub. Clean hair. Warm water.
Two years since we went
our ways, over and over I
turn to the ample tub, the glass-
stall waterfall, the friendly fixtures.
On the road or camping I crave them
like a fix. I remember my life
the way a tourist

back from a Mediterranean
country remembers. I wash and wash. Nothing sloughs
off, nothing cleans windshields, the rear
view. When I shake I remind myself
it always stops, stay quiet, promise
the worn-out limbs
a bath. If someone dictates a poem you have not seen
before, can it seem
a familiar poem?

                    v

Strange as it is, the only thing familiar is this act.
Writing. Getting stoned
with anyone since you is bringing home
total strangers. I thought grass cleared
everyone's daily defensive
fog, brought on its kind
of music. The extra gesture. The flower, the odd
piece of silver beside the bowl. Most often now
I like to smoke alone. I try to care
at least as well
for me as I did for you. I didn't know about
such subtle losses. A light pain
that goes on too long gets
forgotten, becomes an agent, you trust
the familiar face till she flashes
a badge and it's you
in the funhouse mirror. In line for lunch, a woman's
voice above the clatter and starch, "It has
to grow a scab before you scratch it."

Sweeping the Garden

for Deborah Haynes

Slowly learning again to love
ourselves working. Paul Éluard

said the body
is that part of the soul
perceptible by the five senses. To love
the body to love its work
to love the hand that praises both to praise
the body and to love the soul
that dreams and wakes us back alive
against the slothful odds: fatigue
depression loneliness
the perishable still recognition –
what needs

be done. *Sweep the garden, any size*
said the roshi. Sweeping sweeping

alone as the garden grows
large or small. Any song
sung working the garden brings
up from sand gravel soil through
straw bamboo wood and less
tangible elements Power
song for the hands Healing
song for the senses what can
and cannot be perceived
of the soul.

Woman with Child

Sucking the acid
from the disk between my teeth
I plunge to find you child
bewildered in the deep
hallucination
where nameless unspoken
you exist intact before you clenched
your kiss a stubborn mouthful
in your pelvic lip. Ritual

suicide at your parents'
knee. In pinafore
and frilly briefs
atop a table rhyming
precociously by heart *Child
Bride at twelve I was* you mime
a swollen belly *thirteen sons
and by my husband
only*. The audience your parents'

friends laugh
clap and reach for you child
bride body
heat resinous disturbing as you shy
back trip show the lacy
frills. First standing
ovation. You were three. Applause
applause after that act
until you back
hand curtsy. Lifted
from the table thumbs
stray to your nipples lips

stray to your lips they kiss
touch fondle pass you round – arouse
without acknowledging
your passion or the fear
that swells you wordless as a lump
in a throat choked
off. You lose
control. One of them
spanks you. *Without your will*
In pain Through fear the motifs
of your fantasies unraveling already
down thirty years of garden paths
more balls of wool than you can
track back crossed
eyes like pinballs. Small

childbride mother of
myself small hyperactive
lost in a gaslight labyrinth
trust me I bring the kiss
of a desire like
Demeter's her
daughter tricked by pomegranate
seeds. She bit
the clit-like fruit and forfeited
her sex half-live
an underworld
paraplegic. Post-op your eyes

still crossed
you learned about the body
of a god that seen would blind

you light ripping through
the cortical
powerhouse and its dependent
grists. You imagined your spine
alive exploding
vision like mercury
down from the bulbous
matter of the brain. You longed for that
final ovation
of light the brain consuming
itself in understanding and having
understood burned
obsolete. Little one little unborn

child truth is
your body invisible
till now live sensuous
with its reflex kiss. Open your mouth I
love you give
back the bruised flesh
seed. You do. We touch
it trembling with exhaustion
weak. Truth trust
the weakness
of the body. In darkness

now I spit the disk
of acid climb
stairs down
to kitchen un-
familiar instruments
of food and light. Manage the gas

a ring of fire. Take off clothes shoes Tampax clean
our body cold
winter water from the tap three Abyssinian
cats underfoot. Finish the washing. Feel
the slow rivulet on thigh
our blood. Small child I

promise: no more flesh
to chew to touch
the tongue to flesh to pleasure
only choose the few
who know and love the way inside
the labyrinth our body
rocking with relief still
weak by the innocent
gaslight burner. Papier-mâché
and Christmas-lit across the street a child
bride Mary leans towards a manger.
Fire-warmed fogging on
the pane I sit till dawn

breaks child
I have delivered
through the longest
night. Winter Solstice.

Staten Island, 1977

Foreigner

House
Two floors
Down is stove
Down is bath kitchen music
Down is stove and the stack of logs
Up is bed and the climate the tropical
Down is desk next to stove
Around and around floors windows uncurtained
Outside is snow
Unmarked Northern profound white snow
Up small woman alone
Icicles
Naked

Landscape with Leaves and Figure

Passionate Love is Temporary
Insanity the Chinese
say that day
I walked nine miles in the bowl
the hill makes coming round
and round avoiding
the road in
sane I realized a whole
week later at the time
I sank my crepe
soles in the spread
of leaves grass needles
bedding down the path
I took describing
every tree bush fern each
stone leaf stick
isolate
detail in the mind
one woman / it was icy cold / my nose
froze in the air lichen were dancing
up hundred-footed trees the ivy
dirndling up like glitter
flint I stood
there planted
firmly and I could not feel
the cold
wind rain the ivy glinting
savagely like mirrors on the skirts
the six-armed goddess dancing
a storm / wet / it was wet inside
the forest though no rain
was falling it was

sliding
down and you
meanwhile clear
cross-country from the snow
packs of Vermont two weeks one half
a honeydew papaya moon
were eating
while I rimmed the bowl
the woods make in the penetrating
silence between rains in
Oregon in
sane I realized a whole
week later and I said
since you had not yet
left Because
I love you Yes
you said I know that
day

Landscape with Poets

Leaning
over the footbridge the Willamette
River in thaw you said John Berryman
jumped off a bridge like this your
officemate was there he waved
back thinking *friendly*
fellow John
hand raised still
smiling straddled the rail broke
ice

Below
us water hungry
current so swollen it appeared
intimate inflamed

We looked down
river down to sea
so long I held you feeling
a stranger surfacing than fear an ancient species
decimated in the wild wild singing
its last migration down through ice
floes huge emotional the killer
whale the heart

Landscape with Next of Kin

Imagine father that you had a brother were
not an orphan singly that you had a twin
who moved away when he got married had
a kid a similar career whom you had not seen
but heard from frequently for thirty years
imagine meeting him some evening somewhere
familiar to you both not in the village but by
the sea / perhaps / you have

been talking for hours
and for many days
at ease in the proprietor's
gaze – he is young you are old he could have been
a soldier in your regiment that northern province
not so long ago / perhaps he is / you are

here this evening you and your brother seated at the damp
alloy table rusting in some seaside
Patra of the mind identical sighting
the prow of the ferry from Brindisi / perhaps / a woman

bows out from the throng
of tourists very feminine and very strong
resemblance to this man your brother you have never
married / yourself / tonight
are you sipping

the weak milk of your ouzo
having heard everything / at ease / on the other side
of the customs waiting for his daughter your
first blood kin is there anything

in the love you feel
swimming towards him as you did
nine months one heartbeat

pounding like an engine in those waters / is
there anything you won't forgive
her / him

Landscape with Driver

I got my tubes tied on the coast
road to Astoria today it was chilling
driving the weather windy and the sea bright
grey I was alone in the car I was thinking again
I say yes believing you will not harm me having no cause
to believe such things I thought I was being
brave the sea hissed openly the road threw
curves you were back with your father
extending the hearth palm-sized
pebbles in your hands a dull
like your language
weapon

I drove towards the center
for battered women to read my work *believing*
you will not harm me having no cause no part
of that work I had no bruises I kept on
driving hugging
myself around the wheel and driving faster forcing
my attention to the road you were the only
man I made exceptions for believing wanting
to believe we still
could cleave to each other married soul
on soul sloughing our politic
bodies

Banner

International Women's Day I hitch
myself up by the river to the mountains slowly leaving
spring behind and driving into winter
seven hours mist light rain
light snow low light
finally on the windows all
day the sound was either car
or rain or forest then the rustling
metal click and zipper sleeping
bag the tent the quiet then
no human
voice all day I didn't
speak I hadn't sung was glad the stars
did not come out again like eyes it grew too cold
for snow to fall the snow was all
around soon it took over
my whole attention skin and bones
and brain and blood attendant to its duty
the heart pumped loudly I was so
excited I could feel
deeply again and did feel
summoned surrendered to the land
scape slept at last immersed unlimited
in silence hibernating
animals know how
the nerves relax exhaustively
like this before the final thaw

Lenten

Still weeks before the equinox
in March strange pleasure
to prepare to come
to visit you in April April
fourteen strange pleasure not to miss you how
different pleasurable this time
immersed in the collective
memorizing of my senses all
fierce all entangled preparations
constantly at the terminals
at the other stations
in the imaginary the mercurial in dreams
the long lope of a mind
uninterrupted like a raga
drone horizon note against which rivers
mountains miles of landscape and the present
sing

Roadside

Old fir young fir
afternoon indiscriminate
cloudy hard to time
stop the car on dirt
road stretch head
towards the sound of river
oblivious still from the high
way speed sweet sound of river
incessant rising through my ears
eyes I'm clear
across the clearing
before I know the wind
is rising in the branches
not the river very cold
wind very dry
no grass or undergrowth
young pine sparse between old pine
dead branches
all the way across
a path I had been crushing
riblike winter-polished twigs
bone dry

Blockade

The road marked closed
due to snow blockade I turn right to
it goes northeast the right
direction solitary
a thin road
among spare trees rough
macadam a watery sky something sadistic
intentional in how suddenly
one turn and white
floods in the background startled
my mind goes white white as in blind
rage as in white
fury aphasia exile in this state
where nothing is no one resembles
ugly unflattering pent-up
state of annulment
reached too soon
the snow blockade
and not enough just slick
glassy-eyed ice and the rubber wheels

I had wanted to feel solid blockage to
pound kick piss on round out with my fists
grind white on white rub frost
on frostbite some physical
body I could abandon
to

Landscape with Mantra

I saw her at the hilltop
painting and it made me stop
suddenly tired perhaps it was the climb
she was surprised a little at my staring so
I went on crested looked back from the hill
rush-hour light so delicate
in March in spring
magnolia forsythia plum cherry every kind
of bulb a runner made it breathless up and sank
to the ground head limp between his knees
and to the west the light
he could not see
me staring he just kneeled
hands stretched out to the sun
I thought of bedouins of dusk of prayer
in the alley where I stood between
him and the woman cross-legged
on her cushion still
filling in the white
words of her whitewalls words
no one spoke: *con
corde concorde concorde concorde*

Absence of Noise Presence of Sound

for Kim Stafford

The river's blue where it reflects the sky
brown where mountain flat-out long
miles I know I drove them
here

Lean on them silent in the dust listen dry
particles lift to my nostrils
lips

Impossible to tell the silence from the breathing
insects lungs sagebrush breathing in
of winds I here grateful
to be trying

This a desire
not only in the mind
but how the muscle swivels
onto bone how heart wills the auricle
floods and its altered rate

The doorway with the mirror
appears
I have been warned

No wall no door no post no mirror
Still the same highway scooped out with a knife
still the same river

begin again
this time without choosing

I enter pretending it's a dream inscribed dust of dream
stroke stroke sign mountain name a name so excited I wake
myself who had been counting
on that

Oh the dream the moist the scaffolded prepared white wall
dream of a fresco

Landscape without Touch

She has dreams of wolves it bewilders
her how it started with the skin
she put on totemlike one night
now she dreams whole packs and prowls
she prowls
her eye bright mica on the sidewalk
she prowls on bristling phosphorescent slight
she is somnolent by day
she sleeps in light
she becomes one
one less
one less human
one at home among wolves
one palest pelt
one

Still Life

The spoon of desire is crusted
all of my lips are dry
are curiously
dry and warm as all
cold-blooded animals are
warm temperature that meets the air's
grows colder from the skin towards
the reptile center

Amphibian
I feel the air
warping a moist element
oceans of air around the lip
exquisite pink crenulated lip
talc-dusted bloodfilled underwater
lip so pure so
dry

Landscape with Angels

She slept she slept she blanketed
her five-foot-ten frame down with Valium
the soggy gut-impacting down
and slept four days
and nights in a circle screaming
at the angels on their shining
bikes with their singing
chains real angels
real chains
the skull
of god emblazoned on
the dead hide on their backs she packed
herself in sleep
in disbelief
was it her father leaving
again at six at twenty-six
her disbelief at pain that leaves
no bruise the pain of angels
leaving laughing
roars of metal engines chains
in the air like wings
beating and leaving
her unharmed by the police
report angels and devils
black & blue
choirs of annunciation

Prayer with Martial Stance

Days of eyes of eyes
nights of velocities
of insects planets soundwaves
of the brain
days and nights without interruption
green days of chlorophyll light and lungs
water and silence streaming
where no logger trucks
no biker rides I camp
here imagining this
daily discipline
of silence
Silence

Break in praise

Avoid causes of complaint

Change what you can't avoid

In this be

Ruthless

Fast

Since you've gone I've fasted having made the soup
whose recipe I sent (the mail-
man came I wanted to
send something) cold curry thick with oranges
sweet clear onion underneath
the lid. The skin

of this truth's onion isn't
clear. Leathery obstinate I think
how boiled tongue peels simply how it is
the taste buds (cellular abused by heat) that give
way to a larger muscle: tongue truth the matter of
taste and lack thereof the matter of

desire. Hear
me love. I'd do
anything and have to keep this in and you too anything
and have to keep from hearing. Is it complicity
that breeds contempt? Hypoglycemic
fasting for this sense

of desperation forcing me
thin as a needle without compass to let go
of hope and pray for clarity of mind of sky the cold
polar luminary any
finally cold clear star. Solstice
equinox solstice equinox nine months

without desire every time a reason why (ill-
ness fatigue exposure trauma of old
love new love) all true
enough. Enough. I am not pushing

a friendship campaign like you said but love
intense unlimited perverse familial unpretentious

love
is it possible
that it is not enough? Without desire
in a field of stars the cold moon rising hungry
cold lip of a moon the pounding of my hungry
blood the starved

brain screaming *sugar* trembling
at last with clarity transparent lying
in the grass palms joined at the heart in love
desireless in prayer.

Namaste

Gary allow me
    I need to look up tonight
        to a desirable being

Three A.M.   The green
is very private at this hour   Shadowy
benevolence of trees the dripping shadow
rain of branches   Greater horizon
of tree and hill serene relieves
the eye   An artificial
drug they say induces
love for what appears
before the eyes   Consider a room
with an open window   One person touching
herself   Self
sufficiency   In reference
to the substances inducing love the inner
eye is not mentioned   Four
A.M.   Alive
in a city I can walk
stiff-kneed and female feeling
safe   Night
air rare silence here
and there illuminated
glass   Head rests
easy   Infinitesimally
since summer letting down
of hair   No more a pretty
boy
    Deborah
        I'm grateful for this
limber body the Hatha

discipline your heart
which I see beating
equally
well in all you move   All
is important   The mouth makes O
O Praise
O Nothing   Deborah
we didn't know
when we agreed to love
ourselves well for a year
it takes just that to want to
understand
the task   Know
yourself   A Greek
man said that   (I tire
pointing out his mother too
said it proverbially as he
played in the dungy street
of the polis   I tire
of repetition
argument debate
of the obvious)   know
yourself he said and died
corrupting in such public ways
the youth   Another
Greek said anything
that appears and gives sensation
to exist is
real   Greek sounds harsh
and foreign to my ear   It pains me
to admit this of my mother
tongue and haven't

for years   The body guards
its limits   If I sprained my knee
today at final practice if I limp
towards you towards dawn
Deborah because I need and need to feel
my certain limits   Fallible
weak I have wept for this
Joy
        Olga-Maria told me
                I would meet a man
of Saturnine
influence upon me   She told me
I was lesbian by some
mercurial venereal
and watery conjunction   Accidentally
she'd cast my chart for Stephen's
year that bull
headed junction of exact
day/time correlatives in May   Looking at mine
this time I wasn't
lesbian at all she said   She didn't mention
Gary   The Saturn
cycle you and I work
through   The planet Saturn
has been much maligned
informing us as it does of limitations calling
for concentration discipline
restraint of the mercurial
terrestrial the lovely
body   This body
        Deborah of work sprawled out
                six months and nowhere

nowhere was the one
the old crone
wanted and grew white in heart
attack because I didn't
know it   In the dream
she revived
I think   A woman with a needle
jabbed and I
was loosening
her clothing   She had small young breasts like
     mine
Deborah like yours I've seen them
once as you were changing   Wanted
me to speak this
poem and I knew the one but not
by heart   I
       promised   Drove myself
         through Oregon
the greeny garden looking
for the heart felt heart
reviving drone   Daffodil
nasturtium narcissus lily
dahlia crocus hyacinth sweet names
of bulbs I do not have by heart in any
language   Friends
helping   *Magnolia*
one drawled *Remember*
me and the Dixie Dykes   I couldn't
lose magnolia all March   Profligate
indelicate lavender-hearted blossoms
face up side down in
any kind

of light   Day
dusk artificial   Other
flowers   *Did you wash*
your flower?   Does your flower
smell?   Don't play with your
flower   Mother
teaching me hygiene in
French in summer the
language the season of
loved   Love
        Deborah what you say
                you cannot
feel   Lust
passion pity aside respect
this love this friendly
flower   We don't
know the names of things
and still the body
presents us with its dreams   We speak
At breakfast we agree to love
our labor   Hard to keep
apart the work
from worker   Tried
to get around that
woman between me and my beloved
work for months   Gave
up learned to love   The sea
is more important than ever   Who can speak
of the irreducible   A house by the sea
is an honorable
goal in life   Deborah
I don't know if the old crone died

of waiting   Even if
this poem is
the one   Unspoken
healing
            You played flute
                    just out of hearing   Summer
and I too weak
to call   Shuttered and silence-hid
my weakness trapped me like a pack
of wolves traps sheep that will
not answer either
way to *do you*
want to
live?   You bought me talismans
and gifts   Handbound ten leaves
of numerology to teach
my numbers   Eleven you said
was incomplete   La Douleureuse   Eleven
widowed numbers   Migraine
splitting till I'd think
of dying   Not
really but you know
indulging
the mind   You the one I'd want
to call   I have never seen
your body   This cannot be
wrong   I've walked
shivering weak-kneed almost
to your door   In my heart
it is almost dawn   Trucks
stirring   Heading
home   If it feels like love

I told her who was terrorized and disbelieved it
is   I didn't read about three four
or five   I suspect that five is charmed
and sexy   Five fingers   The
Caritas   I'd planned
on seven (mystical
vibration of the body) but it was the time
for what love of the body appeared
palmed before the eyes   The two
crossed eyes   But nine
was union   Female
and male both (*principles*
in the margin) in
a perfect
form   She has a heart
        murmur   Perfect
                Lives
in Vermont   Green Mountain
states of the large
intelligence continuity
of land of being of love   I'm leaving
Oregon in April having lived through spring
once   Twice
in one year
to live through spring   Are there kinder laws
Deborah   Only to you
can I describe her
person   Person   A woman
I and thou like you in
herself   She opens
up she vanishes   She draws
her small tight very Jewish body close she dis

appears   Skinny
people often have
the heart
murmuring as if the blood
too close against the nap made sounds
a bloodsweet river   I have a hole
in my heart Deborah check it
every six months the doctor
said six years
ago
    I was hungry then
        for a woman   Lived in married
student housing she and I
illicitly on sublet couples
in the complex calling
us indulgently young
dykes   Lesbian?
I laughed one first fall night
Nothing to do with my
life   *Nothing   Always*
Lies   I lay twice that year
in student health erupting
hives   We never spent a night
in each other's bed   I had
as always in the past a single
mattress   Only last
    January up at dawn
        the morning she was flying
to Vermont I woke
at home in my own double *having found*
in that language
in which I never loved

a woman *having found*
my person   Greek
blood flows through
my opened heart
less than sweet   I would like to see it also
perfect   The lesson
the lesson to be learned
murmurs close to the surfaces
of the body   She who disappears
Deborah is she who loves
her body   She enters
all doors opens all
windows on lookout for certain
fires   There are no mirrors
in her house no closets and
no key   There is
the garden
out uncurtained windows
knee-deep in snow   Flowers
have names not scents or colors
only   I want to know them
now because inside a dream
my sister said *They've taught me*
words for things I cannot feel   I fought
off evil
words for years tried to feel
her way   My sister was the one I dreamed
of saving   Across the ocean
from the parents – one who speaks
to me in a vocabulary
tentative of love he's never seen
in any dictionary one who speaks

to thank me for the flowers everything
I say to her
eyes is a flower   This too
is a limitation though like your
mother Deborah inert since adolescence
in asylums a
limitation not
solely of the body   If it doesn't feel
like love if it doesn't
feel… Listen
he said to her who lies
for the moment's sake entirely
mutable her blood
incessant rising listen
the doctor said can you hear
where you can't hear it   There's evil
in the world Ramakrishna
says to thicken the
plot   I read that
   Gary
       tonight as I was sitting
on the pot   I knew that would
please you pale
buttocked Gary in the moony night
playing practical jokes
on raccoons   You spoke about the humorous
and other human uses
of manure the afternoon
I dreamed myself a path
away / towards
the garden path of praise
of silence and the wolves (I thought

them dogs then) licking
my neutral blood   It makes some sense
now Gary   I hope I remember
to look for it
again   Light   Still   Before
the dawn   Thin   Upright   Body
smarting still from the discipline   Hatha
Deborah you said means path
of concentrations   Circles
congenital around the hole
in my heart
          I cannot afford
                    to enlarge
the temple   My
work is to confine
its size to force the holy back
into the flesh   I've looked
bright yellow eye
to eye and stood
among them now who prowl
intelligent indifferent warm-
blooded round me   I will
I will stop to live
this
a desire
not only in the mind
but how the muscle swivels
onto bone how heart wills the auricle
floods and its altered rate   Pale slate
the sky the luminous
and iridescent bulbs   Medulla
oblongata   Wet

shoulderblades wet
cuffs skin-warmed familiar
rain   *The beauty of the brain*
Olga she wrote after she smashed the wind
shield with her own just narrowly
protected by a small hard
skull *the beauty*
of the brain is it creates
mistakenly whereas
the heart (learn to live
      with it) the heart
        indulges
in creation   Birds
too have names
in the many languages
I know   I recognize
by call
the crow   I heard birds call before
I saw the light the clarifying
light no longer dawn
of morning   To begin with
any one would do
of the senses   There are six
perceptible in all

March 1978

P.S.

How do you masturbate in Greek
you wrote around St. Valentine's I tried
listening to Keith Jarrett so exciting
to have some memorized I memorize
your letters same variety
of pleasure couldn't tell when
it was over had I come
or not not very
wet I'll come
I wrote in April dis
embodied disembodied
April *All I love*
is always being born
what I love is beginning
always Elytis sings in Greece
in mind in poetry I can begin
again not for poetry's
sake Jane poetry
fulfills you too
fulfill not every
time but over
time beginning over
poetry and you again this
way turn
your face this way
to the light how beautiful
you are

Pastoral Jazz

An idea I had and talked about
became the things I do

JOHN ASHBERY

Naked to walk in my daily Sundays

ODYSSEAS ELYTIS

Elegy

Somebody left the world last night, I felt it
so, last minute, last half-breath before the storm
that hit all night last night drew back. Midmorning
windows streaked with mud like sides of cars. How long

the journey? Sails, the windowpanes the black
thick tarp that kept the woodpile. Dry
Southern wind, in minutes clothes bone-hard, clamped
to the line. Clouds heaving in. The sky, the sky, who *did* arrive

to kiss the eye behind the windswept sheet? Who was it, solo
no longer, shy and desirous to be clean? What song
arose, what crust between the lids
spat and forgot? I woke, my fingers in my eyes

lifted and kissed
the yellow ash, so close.

Body and Soul

There is a joke it goes in Greece
that summer there was a *futbol*
match and the husband had
lost his lady. BITCH! he shouted
after her WHORE WOMAN HEY YOU
BITCH! Greece is civilized
the cop said call your wife
by name. I can't
the man said. Call her name
the cop said. Not allowed
the man said. Call her name I said the cop
said if you don't the man stood in the Greek *futbol*
stadium he said

ELEUTHERIAAAAAAAAAA

Soothsaying

Two coins round my neck, warm coins, lonely
light, full moon beneath the cirrus sheet.
Without you, lonely, happy in each thing
(how beautiful the two small plants are
by the bathtub) plants, moon, light, water
enter me at will. I wear the thin
     flat coins bent for luck, one black

one yellow copper, Arabic script-raised ridges
on each cheek. They touch me, touch each other, rub
abstractions on my skin. No god, but kismet
like a virus rubs its code inside our cells.
The gypsies scrawl theirs in the dirt, twigs,
bird-claws, absentminded laws: here one slept
     with dreams; here one wished himself

child. Jade, aloe in the porcelain light. I bathe,
I glisten. Who knows why. From memory, so far
     away from you, crossed fingers, heart.

Away from Water

Swimmer in the desert
needs to do T'ai Chi, to keep
in shape by moonlight, airstroked,
spitshine on the lip. So dry inside
the landlocked boat to dreamlife. Island
with cypress, idle tongue, cold clit.
Only strong spirit
forms a fist with open
palm. Embrace the calm
calf muscles, flex, all thought
can rush out in the gasp. The martial stars
above you, lazy low-down moon
a slap. Embrace no lap
and love you.

Out of Mind

I manage to forget, distracted purchases or friends
I bring home to the hammock, jazz on the stereo, cream
sherry, slow. Matches, pipe, the light too bright. Indifferent
and glad I get to know them. Sleep, your curly hair
turns white, I weep, I choke the weeping, sleep. Can you
bear to remember? Mornings, a burlesque of light.
I eat, I teach, I run uphill, turn on and swim
or flog the piano, a percussion

instrument that spreads, confounds the hands. I pound
and pound, then hit the hills, again the brown,
sere, beige, buff dunes of wheat, a bristly harvest.
I circle up one, placid as a breast. I run stoned
circles something savage. Solitaire, bright human nipple
on the hilltop, bald bloody sunset, knuckles, bone.

Buenos Días

for Robbie Moore

The things that give such pleasure to the eye, a clothesline
stretched from porch to pine, sixth in a row, eight old
loyal increments I caretake, squat among. The wood splits

easy, tamarack, the axe slowmotion penetrates, cleaves
to the block. The cat is friendly, eats her mice and birds
under the bed. Coyote barks, the old black lab barks back. Dawn

and the wind bows slowly to the shield of trees. Northwest, Southeast.
It's quiet here, windows uncurtained you can see horizon from
horizon. Sunset and moonrise balancebeam, the house at sea. The hills,

benign and magnified, multiply unendangered, field after sandy field.
How beautiful, the farmgirl held the slide of dunes and the Pacific
to the sky, *how beautiful*, she said, *blue fields*. Fields

choking with stars, the beautiful black silent fields each night they mine
me rib by rib and find the bitter almond cloves they fill with honey.

Easter

My father was a warrior, he wore the white
dress with red vest, fez, tufted
hobnailed shoes. He danced
Fred Astaire–thin, on tiptoe led the line
of skirted men to power. Pipe fiddle drum, he charmed a gun
asleep, he heard his mother
once or twice yell *Nicholas!* and turned
quickfooted as the bullet
missed. He dreamed
his mother up through me, his *brujo* dream. He raised her,
dancing pleats a flash, red vest, red head, red shoes eggs wine,
the gyring spitted lamb, so long
he danced, so slow she rose, she rose and crossed
my eyes that saw him split in midair impossibly and hold
      her, hold me close.

Body

Three to thirteen my hair in braids, the clean
tight temples, pale spine up the part. My father
at the mirror, brush in hand, I at the doorstep braiding.
Still months away, mysterious, my blood prepared.
His sole desire to my hair, fierce, chaste.
He wouldn't talk to her for months
after she cut it once.
I cut it off myself
both times I married, veiled
the attentive temples, the long spine.
To spite, to tease, to be and not be his
look-alike, his twin. I hid the woman in his heart
so long I had forgotten. Face
I'm forever about to know.

Host

My father in a dream he lay
thin, narrow, bony on a double bed
and fiercely jabbing
the naked floorboards muttered
Underneath! I shook my head at him.
I didn't understand him.
Perhaps he's dying, I thought,
wants to be buried here. Sadly,
to reassure him of his wish,
I smiled but now he cringed,
all knees and elbows to the wall,
quiet, as if he'd heard me thinking.
I think I frightened him.
It hadn't been himself he meant to bury.

Bride

The sea is known to those who sail it
while those who long for it and weep distort
to hate their own salt, small and incapable
of round horizons. Song of the sea away from sea
engulfs the mouth it drowns in. Who can be happy without cause
to sing? Even in dreams the waters part, open up all the way
one way, diaspora, dust to dust. Some of us give our lives
to study
        the rate at which an animal can unlearn fear
and fall asleep to dream we dream. Tonight I will
to lie down in my native, palpitating
port, to fill
the chill dome of the mind with murmuring, subdued
old florid story of the blood, repeated, wet
vow and lament.

Sea Change

You poured fine sand on me, your swimsuit

fuchsia in the sky, blue moon, gull
on its wing, warm wind. Wet palm leaves matched the sea
whistling and frothing. You laughed above me. Gulls
with webbed feet ambled up
close, their jointed knees
hydraulic, and took off.
You took a picture. I jumped up.
What do you think they're feeling?
Camera slung against the bright
tropical suit, your arms
flanking my belly, leaned, both of us half-on
the unbuilt pier.

The eyes continue to scan a picture

which only exists in the mind, in dreams,
smooth, unself-conscious
bodies of children in an act of play
as if in water, hips in light
green and white seas.
All I ask is to feel my brain, Antonin,
Antonello, father brother counterpart and self,
to lie about on my instrument
in that somnolent way musicians have,
no baton thrust but indolent
lush jazz massages, piercings made
each moment by the riddling light.

If you would stop the girls are waiting

in lavender and green against the sea,
the clouds are cloudlets.
Three ordinary boys, lanky, not too rich,
pass by. The black lip of a frisbee
surfaces, slides, and possibilities
to move without embarrassment,
execute gestures without shame,
palpitate in its wake.
Day after day of cloudlessness, hubristic,
ardorous, imperative: more
and more naked
lie before the world.

Light on the anchored ship at last.

The music of what happens,
white hair on the very young,
the way a gesture is believable
in sleep, the sand, the strip of green,
the universe enveloped in a cloud of dust and gas,
the way in which it happens
is never twice. Forget all you came close to
being to survive. The smallest song
could be misleading: love,
Buenos Aires or eternal life.
A huge red arabesque derived from billboards
turns like an oceanliner in a blaze of calm.

Somebody's daughter is always young. Relieved

of everything, released, as if
I were no longer that
I and she that she, free, discreet, generous,
marking a piece of sky, as if
                              in acquiescing
totally one discovers
an endless movement *sans destin*
et sans destination. A backless
bead dress like a gangway
from the conditioning geometries of pain. *Je suis*
plus belle quand tu m'embrasses, girl
in the light, green and white
sea.

Alibis heap the dreary grounds. Like children

of the filthy and the filthy rich, slick
with the wet glue off the pier, thin little failures
of the will, we dig
a hole and rub its grainy flank.
Just by appearing we create
problems, murderous, poignant,
marring the rails under the chairs,
drunk, and superb, and insensate.
We tangle with the dawn, the down
boldly displayed from some blond vessel,
desperate for the ancient bowl. We fill
with violence and spit, we strip, and try, and fail, and lie.

The broom plants, flowering, conceal the bay.

The child goes underground, whirling and fainting.
A grid of many colors, like the underside of an old rug,
light and filmy, remains. The day is clear, green, liquid.
There are small clay pots
each fitted with a tight cover. Invoking the spirits,
the vine, the shrub, you strike
a pronged instrument that gurgled
once, twice, almost
flooded by some unbearable and huge emotion: envy
of the firmament, that
inlet, that lagoon where our ancestors
instinctively by ear could foretell, perhaps.

Like one who cannot sing but hears

the music faultless, in whose lime-white brain
octopi, saffron medusae
alone some moment, pure, begin to dance,
like one forced wholly
to let out long cries, shame and blush
overcome, one seriously
moved and troubled,
very seriously bruised, purple, ochre
calendars of the blood, whose dark
dense schools rise from the bottom, bottom
up, whose other pleasures, mute,
advance.

Rozan is famous for its misty, rainy days,
and the great river Sekko for its tide, coming and going.
That is all.

That is all but it is splendid. You receive old friends
with new feeling, you forgive yourself, you
who would always live in dark and empty skies.
No choice but a gradual ascent, the silkworm's
passage to Byzantium from China, deliberate loss of all
heroism, even in pleasure. Hammock cords
shake in the light. You sit down
to a common meal, raw carrots,
lettuce, radishes, olives and other things, a place
both empty and set.

Instruction

One must be sitting in one's chair
when smoking opium
so that one will not have to walk
over to it afterwards

Don't light match before filling pipe

Emblem

A woman whose existence is indifferent to yours
attracts you
No music comes of this

no love
orgasms of the earth oneiric
*déjà vu*s for you these healthy portions

field hillock and field
Inside the mind small mirrors and wool
Frames of some wisdom

miniatured there
All the wells open to rain
deep-throated praising spouts there

too   Someone in awe who feels
it ministers out of some greater body
If someone else is hubristic

keen lemon-yellow hurts that eye   In time
a familiar word like *hair* passing between you
enters a desert of camels' bones

Mosaic

Anger violent distraction
Anger daylily of the heat
Anger embellishment and posture

Once (we were separated then) I sent
stones flying to your window in the gravel

Anger accolade surrender
Anger the summer may not end
Anger fill me with clouds I'll cry

night you leaned
out we were magnetized familial face to face

Anger axial eye atrocious
Anger inedible immortal best
Anger fill me with clouds I'll cry

come up you said I did we were
like children in the old boat bed

Anger bread repast emotion
Anger dog hungry dog on leash
Anger in heat! let go! anger enter me

like angels made out of the peacock's sweat
mournful and precious and in sunlight

Anger the simple cuntlip surge
Anger the snakestick glowing
Anger we didn't anger plate of gold

Heart Believes with Blows

A woman sinks to sink it in the sea
Green water enters her scream
salt on her throat like razor-rust

The guilty tire of blame o anger
immense daily decency o art

A woman leaves her ovals on the table
emblems of delicate bitter seas
to scream to plunge and to confront the body

Orgasm

Air
give me some air

Anything
it hurts to write

Truth
truth burns beauty

Home Movies

Far from a you it is always early
Ida at her window   Silence, hard frost
Apples tomatoes figleafs greens
the qualities of shy   In Amsterdam
men looked like you shy
smiles eyes
lowered to conceal
what they caress
The graceful trees of Brussels
the wide open mind
Like long-stemmed ovals feathers leafs
La Drôleuse de Jacques Dillon
Lausanne Milan Mondane Torino
Waking at night I was
weak I missed
you crying
upstairs on the marble
sill – dawn   Cocks
crow and dogs bark early
morning moonshine
patches on the old wall still
Birds call up the mountain of the sky *east*
                              east   Royal
blue silver blue paler
blue   Quilt
fooling the mosquitoes in the heat
head full of sleepless ouzo
Swollen places summer scars   A point
where all sensation becomes emotion

I was mistaken for X by her lover
a British man
white dress and blue dress in the twilight
appearing alike   She put her head in the gutter once
after the rain filled with mud
in agony of someone not yet known
coeval with animals and longing
for the present   tense
The shallow submarine plateaus?
When you will fill me with clouds I'll cry
Natural flow of blood?
Goosehead chopped off
I am not asking you to judge
I am describing to you
PIEROTTO (PIEROTTI) DEVELOPMENT OF
BIRD OF PARADISE MUTATIONS
Times Square
Astor Place
Arcosanti   To feel
without desiring to communicate
in words our own
alien presence
the emblematic enemy
Morbidity of loneliness
of growing old without a god
to hold up the conversation
One might have children instead
Or failing that a school
Or
Lace on the heads of domestics (idleness) forms of
this desire to walk behind
interpreted by the people
like a good wife this

religious desire
My only house is in my head unless it rains

To yield to the sun with a folded sleeve
to spend the day in bed
narrative
as when the principles are embodied
now
to relax all force
and watch the freefall
as though fruit   *What I feel*
not what I feel
about what I feel   (endless endless)
Organically   sin semilla
how *does* a female fruit?
Our moment expands
to its unobserved sensibility
you yourself neither particle
nor wave
O the aesthete!
I put on your shirt because I miss you
You call   You are sorry you've gone
Acquiescing to missing you
I was full of feeling
No you're not   I was glad you called
Chamomile tea clean hair down blanket
black old-world chimneys against blue sky
Without desire slowly feeling
you approach
The sexuality of eyes

The loitering first play
To have no *idea* abt what yr doing
Callused guitar fingers horny
the violin tatooed on the right? left? breast
Drunk on acid
The camels on vacation
The cheetahs were outside
the leotards were going crazy
red spotlight dancing on the neck
Like a steady wicked finger-picked and held
electric guitar-note the string
breaks free
Awe is desire

Does this mean she said
that you're *ours?*

If you tie a ribbon in your hair
if you tie a string in it
if your nightgown blooms with small-stemmed flowers
How wonderful the light is on that tree
just before rain
I can't tell where the tree will bud this spring
window wide open
The moon wide in the sky giving giving
allowing us to look
Aw, c'mon, over-religious water, sweating sea-cloud
slats in the roof the walls the bars
well water in the pan, cold
sunlit disease, a bright

Cabbalah in the air
eye of desire   Erythronium
trout lily or
avalanche lily, deertongue
And how love, the word, melts on your thigh
Wild ginger and Solomon's seal
And the Easter moon that followed us
to our right bright red
How the railroads are rivers here
Walk through the wall into space wise wound
with just a beauty or nothing

As if
the barracuda were
a sentinel of the sea
god's religion
is imaginary
speech   Pearly-eyed thrasher
bananaqwit
ground dove   Subtext of the film
a gold glaze on the skin
an unofficial accomplice
Sometimes I *think* about what I'm doing
color-painted through
that woman   *Orchidée*
It brings something nice filming
Lineal   *Métronôme et* violin
Howard Beach substop
Take AA train or CC train
Mary's house toward boulevard

(right) keys to side door
Bright red shirt and yellow towel
celebrants the south green seas
Variegated couples
walking the shining tides
picking white shells and mourning
Among us
who knows no dying
one?   Air burial
Stray needlework
Maho bay   I choose not to choose
nor to have chosen for me
To follow my course
Rainy and sunny greetings
Meditating off the green tent's porch
more yellow finches butterqwits than human
paired hinged open wide
in welcome to the real
blue against the green
aquamarine of rock
I float about the curls of summer
Barracuda draws close
Zen!
Punk knock on the head!
Life is my roshi

Because the light is so bright
in our part of the country
its absence spells lavender
in the husky underarms

of the sky   Dusk
Spruce Mountain
in its plume of hues
Who hears the bird in the sunset
I love you old
I love you new
I love you all my art
will see how a willow
separated by flowers
stutters
in the broken-open light
All is one you to one
the language of happy
hang-glide over the ocean
boats
circling the Sound with streamers
apples tomatoes figleafs greens
the qualities of shy
Any companion is a guide
a deep-sea river and an August heat
Sensational meaning   as when
no longer one
the beauty of the flower and the need
of the flower are the same
The slightest thing excites and yet
to cast off the Grand Canyon in a glide!
No problemas
Lindos sueños
The sun is full today one lover says
Swallow it whole
Merci

Epithalamion

Our mound of earth dug up
      for a new bedroom
is as graceful as the dunes we drive to see
      The seen
dwarfs our scale   we feel it
      tugging at our brow

and bow
      like guests in it yet we
for bending are allowed to
      sing
some blond dune's surface
      We believe what we see

through the image is the song
      at its source
and so assume the world
      love   shares our intelligence
of heart the natural
      hug   the quick kiss overturned   The smug

like their smiles more than what makes them
      smile
white cows in November meadows
      in the galactic ravines
Venus enters the Bull at birth and again at will
      A door shuts twice

The twelve rings of the night   outposts
      reefs pockets of great abandon what
we expected poetry to be
      as children   yield   As women

we are beautiful for remembering
      how to relax all force

in an unmeasured field
      The moment heals
Out past where the shale you think is
      going to hold and doesn't
silverfish leap from the water
      Tears are worlds not seen

Aubade

She wakes having flown
half a dozen illegal ones

The truth is erotic and shiny
language it breaks

what's small and can't contain
its sigh   It leaves a wisdom that bleeds

metallic
segues idioms red flags in Kansas

She wakes up singing I have three cunts
red yellow brown

copper pennies in the skulls
of Americans

We turn the air is full of sound
golden enclave of hair and blood

sweet perineum
between the two crossed fingers and the thumb

Here we are
breathing together like dolphins

soaked calmed bespattered with the sun
atop the Rockies snowcapped and the whales

they resemble in a mind
snow-lined by pleasure

whole
pastures new like bare feet in the sun

green so young it squints of yellow
true cobalt summer blue of noon

Sugar

I buy what I buy from the candyman
go home and eat it with my honey
Honeyman Honeyman ain't gonna come

Need to spend some time
Need to spend some money
Got another honey young to eat and spend

Oooh I'm bad
Oooh I'm randy
Oooh been bad and randy all my life

Mango in her jeans
Oooh I like it
Odalisque with two cigarettes

Ode

Ask me no more
fame and sorrow how it runs
how bravery is lost
in the hands of the water
It was a flight broad as a garment
wide as the mouth-resounding sigh
legs on a strip of land
halved by a strip of sea
Who was it running day before
yesterday to the neighbors
song axe whose childish horseback heart
a hedonist of storms now frees
The white roots find the wings
warm folded
when you wake next to me
windows slant water hidden coast
Hear our bird
the common song
it ties us hair-hair like a child
absorbing hours
Delta and Delta to the touch
Nile streaming *open open*
Open of opens
which sun sings? which sea
stiff-nippled curly measures?
Embrace me gloss
permeable sound
broad and again tightening
convulsive as the tuber walls
collapse in and then out
Palpable trembling heavily
I lean against your eyelids as your wish

Friend of mine friend of mine
hope earth place light
least evil
moist in the loom of mind
palmshade and waterlily
love
a tongued kiss saturates the eye
See the rose-ocean? the sea a herd?
I turn to you and cherries spill
their blood notes to the teeth
and fill and fall and sail a call
so freshly
loved freshly squeezed

Pastoral Jazz

2 chairs are empty in a sunlit room
O why are you so suddenly so sad
A joy left its ovals on your forehead
Ground fruit is not as sweet as fruit high on a tree

Bright yellow or dark lake
But think of the many-petaled
The pleasant light of daisies in the heat
A fanlike sweep, a mist that flares the light

The very sadness massages me
Afternoons of red wine
The pleasures of penetration
A child overhears and has a marvelous memory

The picture guides but does no work
Days when the dream flows on in silence through the wake
Enveloped in a fantasy of love
True by the dinner hour

A slow dilation sexual of time and grammar
We talk of you in the Redwoods she says grow in circles
Keep in sight all sight
Addicted to ecstasy

A cup of coffee and a prayer
Wouldn't *that* squeeze your breasts!

If I Yes

To be carried
Good luck of skin
Charmed roadside noise
Not to be plucked

Turn to me
As crows turn in midflight
And sketch an ocean
Over that curve of shoulder

With your eye
Sheer luck in Aries
Rebellious mellifluous
Insist on taking out the thorn

Let me be carried
Ribbonlike from your tongue
As if by language
Fabulous

A fathomless interruption
For it is both a tingling and a light
The difference is feeling
The simultaneous inscribe the soul

It will become very quiet
Encourage it
You have an eloquent tongue
Thrum it and it will leap

To its massive shudder
What the exterior beckons
Shape note singing precise plant
Starlight and the mountainous

Psalm grow-up-quick-of-butterfly
Colored wing-spreading eye
A noise cracks and creaks and is a nonsense
A noise is a nonsense cracks and creaks

Glossed shadow mental stills tarot
Black on black lake on lake marble marble
Of women saturated and rich
I have never seen you so happy and

It was good seeing you
My shells, my shy girls
Give me a shadow touch me with light
The dream of my life is to throw myself

The color of Warhol's people
I want to eat my life
Beauty monument design
If I'm not up by 11:30 don't wake me

Backgammon

I slept with Buddha – dog-eyes
everywhere dog-eyes
eager to be blessed

It's lovely and cold
in the southeastern wing
at sunup

… and rub the clitoris modulating
(the throb the shake and the moan)
Of course I love vibrato

entered and flurred
Elegy
if I thought I could lose you

if not why fuss?
How long have you burned there candle
saliva lantern

flame-shaped and fleshy lobe?
The young one's fang of animal recall
A man gets in a tractor

and circles the field all day
half-done
in the mystical silence of distance

assignations in the park repetitions
the place I first touched pubic hair
a shock after the young girl belly

A hint of adolescent vigor
a hint
the corners of your smile

surrounded by the warmth of plants
an overgrown once formal garden
A craziness is always in relation

Dreams aren't dreams that don't relay
Here was a man who loved young women
Here was a woman who loved girls

The notorious bed
birdsong and songbird
The one in the middle gets up

and fills a jug with water
very pleased to be like a cat
not for the sake of anything

The incense sizzles
imaginary cicadas
in the audible
arteries of the breath canal
Heart rests, flesh awnings

I like it when a woman will embrace
her female and female sides

embedded in everything
Odd-tempered scales
the sound of wolves
icicles singing
in the moonlight
moonlight through the prism
purple green
You are free

changed by your own admission
to some other
that would make a simple gesture
understood
A disadherence
of the mind of the wind
awed and amused witness
What made it real for you
is that I said
I whispered go to bed

and touch yourself in her
ear   The keyhole of the ear
sweet voyeur
If I wish to speak
of this as zazen
then it is
my silent mediation
Deerhoofs and pawprints
Tread: tractor and boots
Practice silence about your practice
Horse and tobaccosmell
Completion – you are free

If I think along
the stations of the day
how observe them?
Sweet apples
Mild chill of fall
Harvested and resown seeds
Always to be beginning!
colored by choice early fall
at home in one's bed and blanket
Breast hair, flesh rain
It's a forgiving
It's a kind of jazz
line to its meaning
Meaning you with flaws
Serenade

August 31 performance
Leaves and birds through the silent
repetition of trees
Competition
Play the sax first time
today
mouth full of dream vapors
To get the song out of it!
It's like with making love
It does no good to *remember*
And for desire a peace of cloud
(what you do not turn for
you get)
Fragile for Allie

I lie holding nothing but being
before me
a piece of cloth where without thinking
you arrive
a simple song
to take the mote out of the eye
a handkerchief with daisies
no bloodred haggard cloth
A friend is an absence you play with time
and two friends cheat time
of its morning shortness
white cat a rabbit in the grass
Creek-roll stove-cackle equinox
All loves who loves me

Long history
Volcanic activity in the solar system
Shiny green outfit of some kind
Rare supernumerary arcs
You can have what you want
A little room called love's valley
700 × 200 feet glowing red at night
Fast wink
Slow promise
The dance is the whole big mouth
Rocks on the desk
Shells windowsill
Each scratch on the brain
Ouzo
Honey

Greek coffee
Worry-beads
Oregano
Sweetie
Rugs
A snatch and snatch: joyful moments
Light lapping pebbles
Flat narrow boats
Red yellow stripes
The dazzle of horizon
Poetry is not good
But the desire to poetry
The blue equivalent hills
Of course I love vibrato
Although to dance with god
Is to dance with ourselves
Said the physicist
Violent love so slow it cuts
Cage from around the heart

Imaginary Sufi Garden

for Dara Mark

The first of several good hours
Stove-gazing
Who wouldn't want
The faggots' fiery call

A pair is a breeder's
The past is the future words
Since I know nothing at all I shall be what occurs
And that is the numinosum

The myth seeks to expresss
Relaxation catharsis
As in mathematics a common function
Of real and imaginary

Ideological and libidinal
Hermes the psychopimp

Whose emotions interpret
The calligraphy of the intellect
The bruise astride the star
Petite lecture naturelle et devoir

Sitting under a peach tree in full blossom
Finches jay crow mockingbird and hawk
Honking white geese open cage
The minuscule and pantheistic

Subatomic annihilation
Pulsing with white and red in a splay
Come up without counting!
Allows a being there

Mornings Remembering Last Nights

Stairs arise out of a village
The olive thickets couch the bare
Rock veins
Anticipating a season
A jagged uphill terraced for the goat
Their bearded kneecaps
Yes their bells
Fiction these thickets
As if a flight of birds were always restless
To feel the cold that calls the sands of Egypt
Home and the pungent fruit
Loll in its brine beneath some ship's
Cold and nostalgic course

Bring me a tangerine
Next to a pack of camels
Draw back the curtain answer me
What curled around your all-night lip
No not the light
The light light rollcall up your thigh
Your empty sheet
My absent one my sweet
Was she sweet?
Now did you argue?
The dark and the milky let me lick
High-pitched and fertile without interruption
A human flight of birds
Change is your whim

Hand over water waving
They come with knives now in the dreams
If we don't spend

A morning soon adrift
In promise of music and physical
Like Arabs who were born in Crete
I won't you will I won't you will
Animal skin-flick torture
I let the mornings pass
Footwork of reels jigs and strathspeys
Light of the moon I read a *cathodic* embodiment
The mornings cold maybe very cold
Full of misunderstanding
Eyes startled dice in the crook of sleep

Diagram of Abandoned Mosque

1   The loggia circled by mouths of sleep

2   We startle leaving the garden

3   Medallions of traffic and of steel

4   But phantoms

5   Of circulars evolved by blood

6   Ripple orgasmically still as though power

7   And architecture were not one

8   Except that the wall flower and vine suck

9   The full fruit is its own ripe larder

10 Trust in the care of taste its spine suggests

11 The pit held on the tongue lips like a lantern

12 Though sleep be distant are my dreams less gay

13 Fortunate as the Ferris wheel

14 Sucked shared imagined

15 Great shining steps that train the legs

16 The sunsplit countryside

17 Real and marble quarry with a frieze

18 Half-figures straining the white cheek

19 The great chords of the mallet

20 Women surround us if we squint

21 Florid among the sea wrack

Charisma

after Lewis Hyde

Though customary for a woman
Syllabic melismatic pulse
To set the tempo with handbells
The gift is eaten in a silence

Before the starting point
Three days
After the starting point
The gift prevails and extends over both

Prophetic perfect
A week of idleness is a gift a link
Also a gap
Taken outside as in fantasy

We call this feasting eating wealth
The life of the body is feeling
Once set in cycle it has no cause
Who hears the drummers rolling

Also then hears the green leaf's appeal
Anger like Khrushchev with a shoe
Among the cactus flowers
All other thinking crowds the heart

If I could offer you
A sensation of grammar
Polygynous plethoric no thought thought
Fondles the mind as a mystery

Perennial

In dreaming you have power
A young fox walking over ice
Thursday of love
I break that you may feel inside
My silence your command

Blue sheets are metaphors and glisten
Occasional with milky pap
Your eyes could close imagining
And touch by dreaming what imagined served
Best to un-nerve them

The powder blue of veins the dark
Curve coral opal ridge
You lead
Pleasant intensity
Like relay lanterns eye heart eye

Of heart
Something to lose to gleeful add
Spontaneous applause as in geography
The sea or botany
Pocket without a seed

To drum its castanet so you must clap
The soft skin lining to a hollow
Wind strenuous silk
Hybrid of earth and parachute
Moon spoon

Moon Conjunct Ace of Cups

To be with the one I love
And think of something else
Green bells tied to my pigtails

Open-air latticework
Diamanté sunlight
Cross of sleep

Each time you touch yourself it stings me
Funnybone tailbone pubic bone
Amnesty overleaf

That echoes go on singing
A long time among the shadows
The underglimmer of a resting eye reveals

Ai
Where the overlap gets even more
Tree wings insect wings

Chosen to know them all
Matches in a crowd of fingers
You couldn't even die without them

Where the wound is mental
The first step is stop the petty
This in your physical being

A secret coming out all the time
It's not the wolves it's the sheep!
Fa la la the English

Added to Italian song
Fun to forget about
Where you let go a feeling

Jewel Lotus Harp

Spontaneous singing in thirds
Performed in Lady Chapels
One of the loveliest summits

Blue sky red clit
Exquisitely vocal
A grid half chance half emotion

Most of all you shyly shining among the guests
Forgive me if I kiss your poems
Jagged accompanying melodies

Nature masses
Always in the image
Of the continuous that is

Always in the long run of the easy
Three quick turns and you're lost
Fragmented into practices

A song so simple for one who is blind
Slow maturation
If you could equally well say then say

Deep breathsong for this instrument
Absolute freedom itself
Before you acquire absolute freedom

And an artist an artist has to do
What is really exciting
Beds we made of sweetgrass and magnolia

Petals real not substantial
Our mind soft and open enough
Phosphorescent birches in the night

You cannot rescue whom you follow

A father once so loved his children
To punish them he struck their shadows
I meditate high on a cliff

And float in the glassy shallows
A dream is both
The stone house by the sea

Your early morning flight
Balcony beach-grass sea
I am eight

I complete the rape
Wished for and held back from
Rich unheld feeling

These waters which are not his
Waters and stones too not his in
The water

Familiar to the light
Where you no longer think or ask
Am I happy

Clarity power and your mother
Finally girlish with you
She raises her creamy skirt

To cover her chilly shoulders
Tête-à-tête at the taverna
And orders us five *hors d'oeuvres*

Who taught me dare
And stay in the world
You love and well

Come difference
Indigo polish on the nails
Red tiny mushroom on the stump

Maple and poisonberry
How first you felt the fire
Red tipped from her hands

You changeable and moody sky
And how
To flesh a rose

Only desire justifies

To stop or to turn back
Because your foot hurts?

Sometimes another
Acts a desire
You only talked about

Call this teaching?
As perversion quite simply makes happy
Practice silence about your practice

Always somewhere else away
In your formless
But everything has color and a form

Pushed so far outside my
Skull felt me arch half a body out of my
Sash of acacias

To reunite the infinite with faith
Once and for all before
The lustrust of result

What I have promised myself alone
Articulation
There is no counting the number of narrational devices

Which seek to naturalize
As it were disinaugurating it
The reluctance to declare

Any completed thought
Runs the risk of being ideological
From the purely constantive plane

To the performative
The structure of the functional is fugued
A small-breasted large-mannered woman

A kind of logical time
Counter-logical and yet true
A theme with neither variations nor development

Not directed towards meaning
As in hysteria
Not a sample but a quotation

Four minutes 33 seconds daily
In memoriam

Beautiful form suffices to brighten and to throw
Light on the lesser moment
To and fro goes the way

Whose only idiosyncrasy is being
Especially those who can think nothing nobler than bodies
No angel has refused

What we cannot help both admire
We have no other language whatever St. Augustine
All scripture in vain

Even these one should contemplate and praise
But then deny
She disapproves of me but I delight her

Lake spread over land
Bread to me is that velvet bud
Who was Montale

To prefer conviction to prettiness
To sing out of the raga is to break the limbs of these
Musical angels

Mirabai
Lilavati
But everything has color and a form

How to think without identifying
What are the colors you love?
Almost every other color

Black Holes,
Black Stockings

*from a collaboration
between Olga Broumas and Jane Miller*

for Doris and Sotiri Haralambidis

A cry comes out and is the changing exterior, particles without apparent cause in threes who vanish without a trace. Here and there and where, Moebius space. Who heard suck, who sucked! In the heaven of intuition, a network of pearls where one reflects, where one reflects all others, transient appearances are made. They are made without choice and catch in the netting below or fall through but as through space without gravity, the famous and unexplored falling-not-down. How long they hold there or are absolute elsewhere changes in timeless pandemonium. No one notices probably; probably notices no one. The sea in the distance is now pulling the stars, in the distance at any time and at will, awry as sparkles on the water. What matter! The perfect thing for you here. World polite as it collides, as it surprises. Assume the simplicity of the lattice: in our alternative or became and. And how! How can two of anything communicate so quickly, carried from one place to another like a light-wave for all it seems instantaneous. I seem to see. Therefore under the blue lights rests a girl with a fan and her dress tied under her breasts. She is large, filling half a large chair, looking ahead at herself discreet. Impossible to imagine her not there. The intoxication of the mind is the matter with the body. Colors are outlines with special effect unforeseeable—scarves, capes, nightgowns willing the wind to arrive, imported curtains to part. And one evening half-asleep like a drug also arrives, late, making signs like a crazy person, a violin by itself. So the poppies out of the stone are drawn, curious, to love as to fresh air, waving, aware, complimentary, waking the sun.

The hundreds of leaves inside our dreams also quiver, they quiver, believe it. Like a range of mountains, out of hearing they are earth visited. Bay-leafed, the hands we hold. And on them the maps crossing from right to left, beginning to end. Bodies sequestered into souls. When they are laments we hear them as if they are immersed in water, blurred with tears. And as blessings, if at all. No doubt where I walked as a child, razing the air. If we dare, if we are the cage we painted with an open door, one of the many like a touch of dust in sun accidentally fells the outline with its colored chalk. Little tokens of myth, dream. On a stalk the water lily, on its spring the mushroom, such clamorings on the white pillow! Pass by. Because atop midnight like a scaffolding already we change our mind not sad together, interminably between, flower and fruit. The hexagram which forms RAIN in the sky falls as rain to sweeten the salt water. There we go swimming out in it at the ends of the polished fingers pointing at us, gradually merging into wave. Of the slender towers, gorges, beehives, hermitages, tumbling ranges, waterfields, the sea straddles the globe, more moon than earth, vicarious. One passes with a loaf of bread on her shoulder wrest from the burden of the sea, its great salt lips that search for mountain streams by squatting at the shore or throwing themselves like a discord upon it, familiar but elusive, one of the different women who invite you home as though there were such a place, as though such women find you. They do not become destiny. With their song of the sea, with their timepieces, their waterpipes, they are the hours of the day, the hours born in the alley, the hands taking the glass off the lamp and lighting it. The garlic and peppers hang from the ceiling. The honey and lemon, great nocturnal watches, gold pieces in the other life, whenever you wish. Not much different from advancing, you will speak simply, one word in front of the unspoken.

Remember how close we sat in Sifnos having dinner by the water! You said in your country once you put the table *in* the water. You began the meal, and then, what a great idea to move it over a little, it would cool you, it was that calm. You rolled your pants to the knee and poured drinks all around, the fishbones back to the sea. Lizards climb the stone outside the kitchen by the sea. Weeds and flowers grow out of the stone; relatives spill out of the kitchen. The daughter is well-educated or about to be. She serves us with the happy face of one who is leaving. You lifted your skirt walking home in the dark over the pebbles to pee. One night we saw the only other lovers – they were both fair, she blond and he grey – and their eyes moved only to each other and the sea, these two destinations. Now the sea once in a while slips a wave up to their feet, because a boat passes or for no reason, now the yellow moon divides the sea into fields.

The gods are never the same but remain the same body or rather the sign for it, hearts like pears like beacons. It was only a bird! skirting the salty bands of sea air. You flew. The small good-byes thank you but only because they are following. The large and the best, the ones who must duck to enter, the peaceful black squares asleep on their funny white circles, they will never stop you with surprise. You have an idea in four colors – on the indigo-blue sea with a yellow ribbon around it, a fishing boat with red oars floating on the waves a spiral fishnet orange like hot coals. The smell permeates the whole memory, tickles and clucks and crackles as it comes in the small window, past and able to hurry you toward the beach with good humor. There you are, ever since childhood, that warmer country. As legend says nothing, you pick up the sounds and feel. Turn, the curly hairs waving in the south wind. Turn, the whistling. The plums falling on the fallen blossoms. Freshly whitewashed, the bases of the plane trees, minutes going by. And the flowers in the sand like spirits that close in daylight. Very rested, very smooth, all on the glassy surface patiently. Matter as instinct like eyes gleaming. Equally rare, this massless grace, beautiful white cloud I feel as a child in the blue sky, are the last made yesterday. They aren't personal, nor is one stone on top of the other a temple. The first days there are as one drunk, the vertigo of palaces and villas. The ravine in front inspires a sacrifice, but. Nerves ringing. No background. Riders flung. Eyelids lowered. Waves flash, being chosen. Not thinking, reverberating as eating and retiring for the night. A line is drawn like a tributary and in a circle a garland where, at the tops of trees, milk cools slowly in a footbath waiting for a guest. The symmetry of half-closed eyes along the line of bird flight, and the flags so sure of their movement. The mountain ranges fade that all day lowered bushels of light on prickly trails. I remember when the splendid mouth separates from land and sky, water again as I go out to meet the paired eyes of the fishingboat lights. Gleaming in their heads, sexual, tilt the whirlpool irises, off-centered dahlias, flowering scents confused at the hypotenuse of honeysuckle and mint. Making icons in their saffron and purple robes, in their monasteries, the flowers intend and imply. Beauty abandons the traversed latitudes – seven thousand and seven pagodas the work of people. When the faithful want to pray, when the prayer alights, it is dawn. And, extricable like yellow ochre from earth, when desire spills out of synch it finds you absentmindedly spinning a globe, the bazaars, the exterior lives. Tin the boxes. Gold the rings. Nails, clocks, tobaccos, hashish in its powdered form, dust and cobble in theirs, green kohl, carved scarabs, silk, fringe, garlic, eggplant, chickens, leather, cooked meat, yoghurt, flatbreads, camels, mules, cows, sheep, dogs, parrots, canaries, chess games, old books, candelabra, paperweights, sandals, slippershoes, prayer rugs. Embedded, wedded, the stall to the hangings. Before the snakes are brought out, the Northwest, you see how they will be. Called to, you and I. Isn't the other dazzling! I stood in the high sun looking down. In a shallow bowl lemon light pulled in the wind like a boat onto shore. No other pelago than this when nostalgia seeks a vessel. Tendencies to exist, details expressed, unusual features of the world like the spiral, place next to large public events private ones. Without thinking the meeting took place, prescient; as long as the well-known took to cross, longer was the anticipation, ethos large and in front of me aristocratic. All that I knew imagining went beyond. Churches and baths – churches out of sand and baths when the sea floods in. Beautiful arches like bodies in love and veins of darker sand leading to the water, labyrinthian, hold like cathedral light whatever I say after the fact: energetic mountains beauty tires of; therefore the miracle of the tide accepted. The hymns and the prayers fire, the rhymes air, they are cheering. Breath of god and with two unspeakables!

They drove to the far side of the island. It was rocky and off-season. They found a house with a climb to the bay, and whose nights were protected by its gentle curve. From halfway up they would turn to the taverna lights casting out a short distance to water momentarily released from its journey under fishing boats, whose lights in the stillness went out of round where they entered it. By midday the vendor cries along the streets quieted and the fish was bought and cooked. One lemon to flavor the fish and squirt on the hands to clean. Goats feast on the rind. Bells on the goats in the heat, in the heat bells from the churches. Side by side they flattened out in the sun. Like a sheet in the sun is disinfected, they were, and were lovers who liked each other reduced to very few needs – mosquito netting, a white shirt, a simple meal, rhododendron and thyme steaming in a thicket by the path. They passed it like a gate between the house and the village. The pails with milk hardening into cheese in the cooler part of the house, so round and white, the opening of the well, the late moon – illuminations that come to them in the night, and why.

If we were as ferries and lived only a summer, how lovely to sleep without contact or mediary at the extremes of puberty, the rifling of the beaches where the cheerful oriole names the black walnut, black gum, briar, hickory, white ash. Children spill out of the sexual like flags. One's a goat and one's a sheep. They belong to how fast horns grow, the overebullience of the overturned. Like a lyre or a flute made of eagle bone, the mistral. All appear from one and the same place, elegance, repose informed by choice. Nothing can be harmed in which a sneeze interrupts a dialectic: the darkening sky under which we close in on reality. Therefore the path, though the sand is covered when you say good-bye and turn to go. The reason for toleration rolls to the edge of the water in some mood. Birds in radio frequency, beasts of space who cast about for intrigue, a lovers' misunderstanding that lights the sky first thing. Solarized photo, shy moment in yellow. The pace alone has significance: the artist accompanies herself on a tin pan while the rosebush speaks to its generosity, getting slowly drunk. By the way, by the sea, by the word wait! having its last say. A monkey's remarks among which we arrange our air mattress and lie down for a few hours in the sun, speculating on death-by-longing. The tail of the resentful leads to your door, the trail of the uneventful gets lost half a mile from how a leap is made love. And not taut, not worse, not first, the mortal moment of salt caked to the sides of boats, one or two kind acts.

Like the flesh of Venus is mud, every day is a good amount of time, and of purity beneath every irony, music without ambition, air. How deaf the life of the eyes. Three patches of sunlight in time. The bridge between past and present is that conflagration –first turn! The wind blows the rain off the leaves in the light. Big mind falling into place. How to leave behind one's etc., bold relief. Beautifully muscular, slight belly, milk overflowing stockings at the foot of the bed: Paradiso. I catch myself not breathing; what am I dying to change? The slightest noise makes my heart start. Voice the wide arenas with fruit trees, voice the comfrey and mint, voice the twenty-first of August, voice under the sign of the fool, voice the gods in the hedgerows, voice a hammock, voice in a long-haired rug, voice your father's village, voice depth and serenity made present aster, onions, voice the steaming rice, voice circle of stones, voice wholly one over. What was the passage of the woman carrying eggs across the beach? Dressed in black with a sac on her back, from the bamboo stalks rickety stack. Plastic sac, glutinous, opaque, ovum of night, prehensile her, carapacean, nomadic, wearing slippers over the hot white rocks toward the promontory. A boy rolls a hoop across her path. Old in a cone of light. The hoop wobbles in its mirrored ellipse. It dips into the heat distortion rising from the rock and is saved by the boy with a stick. She shrinks as she walks into the shimmering cushion of air, framed by o-vaults of the passing hoop.

Moon

A finger is needed to point to the moon.
Once the moon is seen, the finger is no longer necessary.

ZEN SAYING

I came across Philip Kapleau's *The Three Pillars of Zen* the summer of my twenty-first year, just after graduating from architecture school. I was a resident adviser at the dorms for incoming "disadvantaged students" and worked two shifts a day at the local upscale restaurant to make graduate-school tuition. I had given myself a year, earlier that spring, to get out from under a terrible depression that centered, or seemed to, on the emotional difficulty of being deeply attached to my father, an orphan who had loved me consistently and deeply as his first and only blood kin the length of my life, and being appalled by his decision to remain in the army in the context of the military junta that had seized power in Greece a few months before I left to study in Philadelphia, a junta that was, each day, torturing friends of my friends and dividing, once again, my country. I had vowed to myself that if I could not find some joy in living at the end of that year, I would kill myself. It was a calm decision, unlike other of my histrionic attempts at resolving inner conflict.

My most significant religious influence to that date, apart from the generic and mostly cultural Greek Orthodoxy I was raised in along with almost all other Greeks since the Nazis had pared down our populace, had been the Hasidic concept of serving God through joy, through acts of a whole and integrated self, with sin defined as any act of divided intention. I felt completely divided and, in that division, completely fallen from the grace that constituted, for me, a deity. I read *The Three Pillars of Zen* and began sitting zazen. I either did not read, or failed to retain, instructions about limiting sittings to a half hour twice a day. I sat for almost all my free time, hours on end when I had them. Soon I began to lose my sense of continuous self, to go for walks and become what I looked at, to find myself in strange parts of town without memory of how I arrived there. I was frightened – the university was in a dangerous part of Philadelphia – and also thrilled. As a child, my dearest solace had been to look at something, usually the sea, until I became it for a spell, however brief. A stillness began its hold on me.

I moved to Oregon for graduate school, found the courage to drop out of architecture – my family's and culture's choice of an acceptable profession for a well-brought-up girl: one could practice at home, among the family – and spent a year working the heavy limestones in the lithography studios until I found that I could study formally what I had done privately since childhood: write. I read more on Zen. I sat as best I could. I heard of Gary Snyder and his statement, graduating Reed College when he had been my age, that the most difficult discipline is that of following your own desires. I read W.S. Merwin, whose directness, depth, and simplicity seemed to me unimpeded utterance from inner-most song to God's ear. In us all. I heard they both practiced zazen. I had company. Since then I have deepened daily my attempt to "sweep the garden, any size," to practice what I may conjure as belief and keep the words about it as closely limited to song as I can. I don't trust words that are not linked, through the music of poetry, to both sides of the brain, to heart and soul.

My most active desire, having been carried in the womb in the bloody aftermath of the Second World War, having been raised in one room while the adults told and retold the forced marches, the missing frostbitten digits, limbs, the humans missing from our fold, the executions carried out by the jagged tops of tin cans opened with those old-fashioned implements still found on Swiss army knives so that "it took longer" – I was maybe three when I heard that in the soft and bitter murmuring in the circle of light around the table just beyond my crib – my most active desire is for peace. As best as I can define that, challenged by a workshop on Nuclear Despair and Empowerment where most of us came up with static definitions hinging on the absence of war, is that the active state of peace is healing. My garden has become the human bodies I can touch, in love, respect, and silence, in my daily practice as a massage therapist. I sweep and sweep and am incredulously thankful it is possible to thus construct a life. Poems rise from that sweeping and are held in memory for a time, then written down. Everything else is the spirited noise of this world, this time, if I am still enough, even the dying that surrounds us now in our small, gay, fishing village where more than a quarter of our people may be infected by AIDS, mirroring the terrible suffering everywhere on the globe. I have no hope, nor absence of hope. I have the sweeping. I bow.

Perpetua

for Rita Speicher

and in memoriam
Barry Binkowitz, M.D.
1959–1987

Happy who has seen the most
Water in life.

ARAB PROVERB

PART I

Mercy

Out in the harbor breaths of smoke
are rising from the water, sea-smoke
some call it or breath of souls,

the air so cold the great salt mass
shivers and, underlit, unfurls the ghosts
transfigured in its fathoms, some

having died there, most aslant
the packed earth to this lassitude,
this liquid recollection

of god's eternal mood. All afternoon
my friend counts from her window
the swaths like larkspur in a field of land

as if she could absorb their emanations
and sorting through them find the one
so recent to my grief, which keeps,

she knows, my eyes turned from the beach.
She doesn't say this, only, have you seen
the sea-smoke on the water, a voice absorbed

by eyes and eyes by those
so close to home, so ready to resume
the lunge of a desire, rested and clear of debris

they leave, like waking angels rising
on a hint of wind, visible or unseen, a print,
a wrinkle on the water.

Evensong

The silvery leaf of insouciance lifts off the bay past dusk
and with it, like breath
or the barely visible exhaust
preceding nuclear explosion, dazzling,

the sand shifts deep below the house.
I feel its tremor in my ear, pillowed
on the futon on the floor,
and through it other tremors,

Soweto, Palestine, the lower
American continent whose beauty and bounty
enervate our ghetto-bound conscience.
I float on my freedom my sleepless nights.

The bay, underhem
of our planet, link to my natal beach, blue algaeous pinafore
home to whale and fleet,
no longer rests me. On it, the spit

of the Arab touches me,
the venom of the dispossessed inoculates me,
the vomit and sweat of the detained, soaked
into earth and filtered through it,

tenderly meet the fine white sand
as if what remained of suffering to speak
were love. I am held
in the field of my freedom,

for which I exiled myself as soon as I could,
blind as though a corneal membrane,
which I coiled all my life behind to break,
let in only intensities of dark and light,

and freedom was light shattering
the mesmer of high noon in the Aegean.
Held there, my body weeps,
meets these marine broadcasts with a sadness,

dry, spasmodic,
elusive of CAT scans and sleeping pills.
By day, I ask of those who come to me for answers,
what would you say, asked by a poet

whose tongue and nails have been removed, whose nipples
are cratered with ash, to account for your freedom?
Seize it! I urge,
and return by night to my seizures. Peace and serenity

are the temple I shape, whose officiate,
joy, is choking.
Some may be seen beating her
on the back with clubs, others

with tubes down her nose enjoin her to vigor.
The beauty of strawberries,
organic and handpicked by my neighbor,
in the blue bowl by the open window under circling gulls,

is likewise insufficient to rouse this Demeter from her bane.
Daily I make my offerings,
nightly receive the clash of the objectors,
those who squeeze tissue salts from humans for their brine.

Like a pit in the fruit's ripe stomach,
encircled by airborne toxins clouding its permeable skin,
I am nourished, gratefully,
by the force of an unconditional

habit still linking life to the pulp of fruit.
Gestures of offering, smooth forearms of receiving,
between them the vivid colors of rare untainted food,
like a brooch with its gem,

are the medals we're known by and carry, how long,
into disarmament, to joy's free breath again above our heads.

The Masseuse

Always an angel rises from the figure
naked and safe between my towels
as before taboo. It's why I close
my eyes. A smell
precedes him as the heart
fills from his bowl. I bow
down to the riddle of the ear,
its embryonic sworl nested with nodes
that calm the uncurled spine,
a maypole among organs.
Each day a stranger or almost
crosses my heart to die
from the unsayable
into the thickened beating
of those wings and we are shy.
Or frightened as with clothes
on we forget
abysmally what heaven
shares with death: what gypsy vowels
unshackled from the lips
rush the impenetrable
mind and the atlas
clicks in my trowel hands.
Crocuses on the threshold's south
side then and now. It goes on
like an egret scaling the unruly bands
of atmosphere we have agreed on
by my palms'
erratic longing of the flesh
to try. Toes crack. Hips
soften and the spine,
a seaweed in the shallow spume,

undulates like a musical
string by the struck note,
helpless with harmonics.
Rock. Cradle the perceptible
scar of the compass, sensible
stigma in a poised blind
of trust angling for reentry,
and the rain, the wind
across its face like minnows in the dark
of love schooling the light
will speak to you and you will walk
home dizzy, grazed by the gloaming and the just
illumined stars.

Stars in Your Name

*All day you stare at us
who may not touch
your weeping or your blood.*
HEATHER McHUGH

Kind, kind,
milk in the mind,
milk in the child,
child in the blind

hormone of sleep,
at night, supine
anchored paralysand,
flat as a star

soaked in the hopeful calcium
all mammals
like a prayer paging god lie down
to weep out for our young, mild

soporific milk
endure our cry
issuing ineluctable
and somewhat like a bird

in flight out of an oil spill,
a black bird that had just been white,
a brother from the cratered tit,
aureoled, blue, perennial,

in orbit in the buckled sky
o soul on its invisible
tether from the dippered
water that was self, now

rise through the historical
ocean-skin that divides
the dreaming anchor from its days, each night
a nipped rehearsal for the unrequited

vessel filling, filling in a child's
mind since the shock *unfair*
took it by force,
unfairly into concept,

and Justice, signal star,
tore from its center to abide
above the ferns and shelters
where in dreams a life

soars up to lick the fabled light
from its inverted triangles,
paired fairly in the sky,
glowing from our perspective

a phosphor that might nightly heal
the hole in the clay
flowerpot and brim
the unknown nourishment that balsamed

angel with open eyes, untarred
and gleaming-feathered, lets
our solace be your
flight.

Mitosis

Resist anxiety
itself the making beautiful some abstract
you
in the continuing light
perennial water moving
its overwhelming percentage through
us its visible tide
unconnected and unified

to be alive

you said
time embraces
as we embrace behind the white
window-door meters from the bay
in our sideways fashion
and the exclamations
bright trumpet-flowers behind us
in later memory
that evening say
you out I in
adorned

solitude and affection

rarely
even if every day
the heart moves in its little
sideways thrust over gravity
to an exalted place composed of ringing
pitch so exact
inaudible it sweetens

the air whose luminosity
amber sweetens my lungs

memoryweed

burning at noon on the island hills
invoking a natural theater
where the arenas of possibility
are enlarged
in the speechless intense camaraderie
of instruments when their players
without ceasing their music

leave.

No Harm Shall Come

to my sister journeying toward
            me with her piano
fingers capably
                    spread over her child
    as she holds him
        to herself in a front aisle
                    of an airplane over ocean.
            She is leaning
neither forward nor back.
                    She is joking
    with a steward
and she has taken off her shoes and feels her feet
                larger since birth
        spread on the fallen blanket a sensation
    she enjoys
and turns to her window
                        like clouds.

        Last week a friend of great intelligence
    and compassionate beauty said she'd not feed a son
            from her breast
                because where
        later find that enveloping orbit and why
    introduce the need
I disagreed
    but she would nurse a daughter
                as she in turn could nurse
        and something terribly awry
    and black got twisted in my lungs.

Later talk turned to Sophie
                  and the incalculable guilt
                  of the survivor
            child chosen by a mother
      under the extreme duress of the trainride
                  and the hissing name of the place
            chilling us still.
      To refuse the guilt is an act of life,
                  we said, at the time I thought Life.
            It was outside the restaurant.
                  Snow was falling.

Eye of Heart

Because I was whipped as a child
frequently by a mother so bewildered
by her passion
her generous hunger she would freak
at the swell of her
even her love for me
alone in the small house
of our room by the Metropolis and fling me
the frantic flap of her hand as if some power
in me to say *I want* brought the unbearable
also to her lips

and as it didn't hurt
nearly as much as her distress
imagined it and set the set I grew up longing
for consummation as she did
beyond endurance
tenderness acceptance of the large
insatiable that grows so small
and grateful if allowed
its portion of sun

so that the images that led me down
the spiral of forgetting self and listing
like a phenomenon in the grip of its weather
dazzling or threatening but free
of civilization were the links
whereby her terror
made good its promise to annihilate
my will her will I couldn't tell
the difference then as now

when making love I can
breathe in forever on that rise
indefinite plateau whose briefness
like an eye is unself-conscious and the sphere
of the horizon its known line.

After Lunch

The PX wives who smuggled the dinette
set for my mother on Stadíou Street in 1956
sleep under their cilantro plants poolside in Arizona.
I sponge down the Formica, lay the cloth and run
out to the car. It's not that far
but straight onto the mountain. It's a scar
among the dwarf pine scrub, bulldozers on each side,
the three-winged gate arching alone, a filigree of concrete,
the turned earth red, frank to the sky.
My pumps leave tractor imprints, it's the fashion,
snakeskin finesse and Vibram sole. Here, she says,
a corner lot, a jaywalk from the chapel,
florist *en face*, a cosmic spot: she means
socially advantageous. Her best friend's over
there, by the far wall, terraced into abstraction.
They all admitted it, she says, I drew the choice
plot. Midday at rest
buzzes and ricochets. She shows me where
the flowerbeds will meet the promenade, her word,
and then, the wild oregano
fuming above the future
graves, we go.

Périsprit

In the hospital, in the impartial beauty of sunlight,
he tells us, *Do not weep. I don't know if I can*

come back, but if I can it will be through your joy.
Historical earth too small already to contain our dead.

In four years I will lead my mother to find the priest
walking through the garden of graves. He is ready and she

does not walk with us behind the chapel where, unearthed,
an armful of bones in a tin ossuary bathed in red wine

is set in the sun and the long night through evening
to another dawn under stars to dry.

On Earth

When we drove up to the curb the woman
in the dun-colored house stained by the rain of days
when this was a village beyond the city
came to the gate to shrilly
claim the parking space.
She argued with my mother, unpacified
by the steady line of the wall
and the small rear entrance
we needed to reach
across the street, but my mother
mildened by it said "half an hour, half
an hour" and we crossed.
My uncle was there. I held my sister
and then her husband wheeled
his motorbike along the lane, helmet in hand.
We waited for the man
whose job it was to see the bones were ready.
Sometimes the flesh is slow:
sometimes a daughter buries her mother
twice in the reddish earth as mother had.
All the allowable extensions
having passed we waited
holding a bottle of wine. The priest
came to take it saying
it was good, the bones
were dry. Uncle and I
followed him to the washing house:
a dun marble sink through the limed
doorway – by its step
two ossuaries stop our feet. The priest
directed my attention gently
from the smaller bones
I instantly chose as father, dapper, petite, lithe

dancer in uniform at Easter, leading his
circle of men, to the raw and bold
armful deeply stained
already by the wine. Earth, blood, vine.
We said a benediction. The widow
of the small-boned man held up his picture
and his ring. He had been bald and portly.
Through the heat,
the moisture rising from the sprinkled earth,
the crickets and the flies and bees, the distant
scrape of digging, the thin
voice of my sister rose
and rounded the chapel to meet me.
I held it so it too could see.
Good bones. Thick bones. Bones drinking deep.
I carried them,
with the woman whose job it is,
farther behind the chapel
for their day in the sun and vaulted night
and wrote a number on the box in Magic Marker
I gave back to the woman with a tip.
My uncle was telling a detailed story
about his alarm clock and how it broke
and he returned it to the store and got a new one
thirteen months later with a new
guarantee. My mother, his sister,
listened to him. We walked to the front
gate to sign the papers
and back past the famous Sleeper
that drove its sculptor mad by never waking
to our car and the quiet
landswoman eating the noonday meal
with her husband, his truck pulled to the yard.

The Pealing

As in a parable the truant father
arrives. The birth
attendant there and I
distrust him but our panting

friend accepts him and we three begin
with her the three days broken
in portions of seven
agonizing breaths

and the uncounted minute
and a half we sleep
between them like a heart
rests calculable

lengths of lifetime
between beats.
Each third and fourth
breath brings her eyes to panic

so fierce her head tilts
on the axis
her eyes locked into mine
and once again I am

inside the camp
the peaked cap
and eyes implacable
and blue with pleasure.

Souls rose up with the smoke
and settled over Europe
as now the random hot
spots of Chernobyl.

Some say the hippies
now the Greens
are these souls born.
I recognized the Jewish toes

of Esther, the scholarship
girl from Athens in the pool
at the American Consulate
cocktail party honoring the brain

drain we were part of
and bent to kiss them in the stupor
of that event before her
eyes held mine and we both

stopped. I live
since then with Jews.
I leave the room
where my Armenian

friend exhales
and sleeps for ninety seconds
and rouses and breathes and screams and sleeps
her third night

before dawn
to weep. So many
born. Such
natural pain

and still the clubs the whips
barbed wire cattle prods napalm
Klansmen and Afrikaners.
On break a midwife

talks me down. On Demerol
at last my friend is sleeping
deeper between pains.
I cross the hospital

to see another friend
and help him shift position
and suction his mouth and hold
his gaze. "White cars," he rasps,

"bridge sky." Twelve hours
to his death. Equinox.
March flowers
lunge in the heated air

petals omnivorous, pistils
throbbing. I make it back
by noon to tell him it's
a boy. The head spilled

blue, cyanic, ocean blue
in flat dawn light, pale blue
and sudden in six breaths and Beth
stopped a long moment

as in strobe
elbow to knee
inscribed dark totem with two heads
one fierce, one blue.

The obstetrician slipped the cord
loose from his neck
they howled
he flopped

rubbery and engorged.
Plum testicles:
waxy, veined, seamed
still to the tree.

Parity

This side of the post-
apocalyptic treason I

pledge allegiance to the infant
raising its spine above the sand

of history to fit
its genitals to it to reach

from hand to mouth
the bitter sun-encrusted grains

it sprays back from its gums
mixed with its blood and spittle

on the adjacent sea
calming the spot of midday surf

time and again with glee as with
a seasoned fisherman's technique

of olive oil flung with sand to still
the trembling water.

Eros

On Death's face all religion dances
like pins on the head of a clit
and from that ground draws its defiance.
The nuclear menace can silence us

if we are atheists or lead us to think so
but here's Death, at least, behind our shoulder standing
as the not-without-which of the nightingale's
ability to thrill us past midnight

willingly on a south-facing slope.
Atheists plead insomnia.
We reach past sunlight to its savor
midnight recreation of noon like helium lift

midbelly, luminous, melon-bright like its satellite
counterpart in some phase in the skies, in tune,
full face to its provider of heat.
Therapy, healing, the active

state of peace roots in summer, and harvest,
war's opposite, in heat begins its ontogeny.
In sex, the eye-slice of my head
dissolves as bay and sky infix

in the face of and because of what
we do not know, won't know, can't know
and would rather our eyes melt down
our face, our mass

irradiate in instant vapor,
our shadow implanted on the molten rock,
than know. We love
while oranges absorb their deadly ration,

the wheat is withdrawn from our markets,
the Pershings carry their sixty madmen
like clone Persephones half-lives beneath the sea,
madmen jogging the drab green

bays of the submerged bullet in drab green, a drab
meal microwave-silent in their gut, earphones
plugged to pillows, also green, on generous
coffin-sized shelves from which the meat

is long due recalled and most of them
just past eighteen. While the chickens
are bred without claws or beaks for easy packing,
the bluefish, striped bass and perch float up

cancerous, while the President
eats the last hormone-free meat,
while the Holland Tunnel smells sweeter
than Paris in springtime and emission controls

are still being repealed,
while thank god the Dutch young
push their antidote for apartheid, only a word
like a song badly needed around which the lips

of the heart with their hunger can suck:
vrijheid, vrijheid
and the new Rainbow Warrior leaves their harbor
for the antipodes of defeat.

If I just have ten days I will fiddle.
One hundred years is as short.
Swell my strings, thump my drums, faith
like orgasm is problematic in the mind,

having no currency to bank. Its current
must be seized to be. When I'm risen, suddenly
past my brood of errands and their constant talk
like that of children a mother learns

out of love, part time, to ignore –
beer, bread, holy beard of an organ
that shrinks and grows psychedelic as Alice
in Steinian wonderland.

Even grammar sprouted tongues eager for that face.
Tender cows, holy buttons.
Gertrude the dervish in a field of words,
encoding the dogma: strategies

for prolonging pleasure are the faith
of oxygen fucking the lungs of life.
I believe the explicit is its own shield.
The godless see metaphors

while the born-again daily are
to dally among the miracles.
Why else be given astounding organs.
Why else given jungles where the improbable

not only grows rampant and awesome but provides
a good percentage of the globe's oxygen besides.
Amazon basin. The text
of sex, word for word and by heart

divined, enacted
in the antechamber of the soul so kindly
also provided me, is my guide and prayer.
When my skull shears and the sky

fills in I'm found.

The Massacre

I understand Xerxes' command to wield the whips
on the intractable, bereaving apron of the sea.
I beat the foam with racquet and with bat
hoping the tangled plant
in my therapist's office will escape
the havoc of my grief and when it thrives
from week to week increase
the fervor of my sickle
arm soughing the calm
air in her witness. A murderous
growl like a machete flattens
the delicate bronchi where the lungs
come to a stem. The ghosts are with us
poured from bruised tissue like the blood
I spray, embarrassed, on cream sheets. My scream
is tireless, my arm its pump. I hate the arrogant
poet who last night remarked
how much the natives recollect their wars
beside the birthplace of the ancient
memory he came to paste
onto his suitcase between Rome
and Istanbul, Berlin, New York, a gaggle of invaders
around the nameless, dusty, unmarked shore
young Homer roamed. Suitcase rhymes
with exile only for a native. I had to learn
it rhymes with the Bahamas for the touring clerks
who keep the books that feed on distant, ill-
remembered war. Two Germans walking home one dusk
cracked a boy's arm
across their thighbone like a faggot
and threw him on the pavement

writing. It was fall. The fabled
light of Athens shone
on the protruding bone. Their boots
were new. They raised
the infected dust and in the silence
of the boy's disbelief and pride
the untold eons hide.

    II

The friends of the dead lie on my table.
I do what I can
with their breath and my hands.
Witless, the birds are singing.
The crocus-garland month lengthens our light.
I want it
always to be light. I fight the night
and win. I peel my eye
against the black and white
TV until it dawns then sleep.
The Palestinian and Boston
homeless split the screen.
Number of children living on Brazilian streets.
What is forty million? Jeopardy's prey still the camera
their stripped and stunning faces
emblazoned in the halogen
a kind of sustained lightning
and the peasant heart
who counts the seconds between flash
and fall of thunder shrinks
from the looming toll.
Horror is toxic.
The lesions

on our organs keep the score.
The gentle and the hard are being taken
in legions and the globe
might shake us off its flank like quarry dust
and start again with something less
free, less
wrecked by greed but it suffers us
on its blue cetacean patience
like festered barnacles.
Like counted sheep midair over a stream
the friends of the dead pause on my table.
The shofar is ringing like starlight
too young to have reached us.
I do what I can
with their breath and my hands.

III

There were bombs in the womb, pulsing
the dark with adrenaline, stunning
the skinless swimmer, fusing
resistance to the bone.
The body of my mother
likewise was carried home
in pandemonium. An even score
of generations swam
through bootcamp to the shore
of first light, freed
to fight or flee
the random detonations
of Pasha or Nazi whim.
Only the land, the home
invaded, raped in, lit
like straw gave up

the rubble to rebuild.
The tongue
our tongues were pierced for speaking
moonlight bright, shine all night
help me learn to read and write
rose from the fertile
ash. Whole men
were roasted on the spit.
The gatherers of children
roped them in.
Women would rather jump
in the ravine than breed
the bastard offal.
Rinsed hair and aprons
dripped a serpent
path from well to rim.
I understand the urge
to beat and maim and kill.
If I were Black,
which I am,
if I were Jew,
which I am,
Irish, Palestinian,
native or half-breed,
which I am, I am
homeless or disappeared,
immigrant or queer –
Resinous weeds
grow taller where the water
dripped on the craggy slant.
I pound the mattress.
What I don't understand
holds us back.

The Moon of Mind against
the Wooden Louver

The visitors in room 8509
stand in a circle chanting something Russian.
The Hassids down the hall have come
in segregated silence, men
roll their thick white stockings in the lounge,
mother and sisters still
between the door and bed each time I pass.
We step across invisible or merely transparent
shadows making up their mind
to speak, to intervene, to cull.

A firm hand – like the A.M. nurse sponging the last
few hours of confusion
from the somehow childlike
emaciated limbs and face she lifts,
a bride, I swear, swathed in a sheet,
back on fresh linen and then clips
the bottoms of the flowers
keeping the family at bay while Barry naps
in her unbridled trust – we lack.
Not without prayer. Not without

the pluck and humor of the song
your bones thrum while the blood still laves
their broadside and their flank.
I kiss your bones. In mind
each rounded pinnacle
of rib is white
against an O'Keeffe sky and light
their lingua franca. Such thinking heals

the moment. It divides us
for its duration like a cyclone

fence from our despair, our rage, our bitter greedy fear.

Touched

Cold
December nights I'd go
and lie down in the shallows
and breathe the brackish tide till light

broke me from dream. Days I kept busy
with fractured angels' client masquerades.
One had a tumor
recently removed, the scar

a zipper down his skull, his neck
a corset laced with suture.
I held, and did my tricks, two
palms, ten fingers, each a mouth

suctioning off the untold harm
parsed with the body's violent grief
at being cut. Later a woman
whose teenage children passed on in a crash

let me massage her deathmask
belly till the stretch
marks gleamed again, pearls
on a blushing rise. A nurse of women HIV

positives in the City
came, her strong young body filled
my hands. Fear grips her only
late at night, at home, her job

a risk on TV. It was calm, my palm
on her belly and her heart
said Breathe. I did. Her smile
could feed. Nights I'd go down

again and lie down on the gritty
shale and breathe the earth's salt
tears till the sun
stole me from sleep and when you

died I didn't
weep nor dream but knew you
like a god breathe in
each healing we begin.

Walk on the Water

Chafed ocean, a chadored moon
fluting the supple acres,
the silver spine of surf drawn from

a shore still resonant, each sounding
molecule discrete yet filled
with sameness so continuous

we might believe you too
though drawn from us instill
us who are left

with eucalyptus resin on our fingers,
after the flowers,
torn from Styromoss,

have drowned the hollow grave, its sound
of metal against bone, although
the earth was rained on, soft

the hands on the shovel as if one last time
your arm – peace
is that continuity,

you were trying to tell us,

faithful and loyal to the last
you were cast from, friend
in the vibrant elements,

song without skin to hold.

Before the Elegy

for Paul

Midbay, the Nikonos,
a pun on the bright island
of my childhood, sinks
its waterproof housing
guided by hand not eye,
to the burly and the slight
blond figures casting through
the wide-brimmed net
of light against the bobbing boat.
The frightened photographer is brave.
Shut tight, her eyes
relinquish to the skin their grasp.
They surface, all three
explosions of lung made light
and drop again to fly
arms wide
two dancers and a feeling eye
into the dolphin-liquid dark
that holds them as a bird in sky.
More, more than we believe
gives light.
The hair, the beard, the nimbus
on the glans, the sheath
around the plummeting,
the seaweed and small fish
are stars against the lapis night.
Stretched out
across the screen the slides
force us like ocean to hold breath
on land. We hold,

the slight-built German and his wife,
the large blond man who rowed the boat,
the artist and her girl and I,
illumined by the tangible
dream of the flesh made kite.

Native

Driving with mother to the shore,
northwest then south from Athens,
deep black and straw-gold earth
arched with the white ejaculate
the mobile force of irrigation,
to a mountain pass,
as through a mouth,
iron-red cliffs above
my father's village.

Olivegrove, poplar, silverleafed
the stark descent,
as if his soul had pared
the way through these
benefic mountains,
ridges receding in a haze
of heat over the omphalos
at Delphi.

Adelphae, siblings I and she
in the irradiated steam
of thyme around that belly.

Rust earth, mauve sea,
zigzag at zero altitude at dusk,
mesh-aproned hills and bell-flocked sheep,
home stretch.

So much of that
acreage and livestock was to burn
in August's tilt from rain,
watering wheels in charred fields without hoses.

We bathed in the sea
by the house they built,
two weeks unsnarling the garden,
dahlia from bougainvillea,
arguing only how much salt
to eat at last.

After *The Little Mariner*

I woke up in the dark
of a moon steamed against glass
black as if glazed with ebony
or soft lead handled in the blind
of another's dream and he
the crossroader
the atmospheric horseman
the marksman who can calm the deep
by taking a teenager

down from his constellation and instructing
him to walk across the surf then kneel
inside the pelago a broadcast
charging the elements
with Rilke's terror as my soul
rang in the air above
the bedclothes rustled though my limbs
on the bed were paralyzed
transparent

I could see
a ribbon song begin
from the lungs of his penis
inside my body like a swallow
of ice-cold milk in August
gleaming and slow like mercury
upstream and through my lips
and then my soul
fell into or my body rose.

PART II

Amberose Triste

Beautiful sex whose lips I know
hasten to light and deep to darkness

shaven from your lair
where

in the lateral maternal
blue by California

chill now
your amber drink and smoke.

Lengthen in repose
as the evening on its way

from me is apersonal
your matutinal

leap into dawnstruck light
from the sated Atlantic

a planetary motif.
Salt through the earth conduct the sea

skull, patient surface.

Next to the *Café Chaos*

the lambent cobblestones refract the blue
and yellow of *L'Afreak Électronique*
into a frazzled dayglow
batting the piss-crossed wall that jogs
the curved canal from *Milky Way*
to ambient *Paradiso*
regulars spiking the street.

Under that blinking sign,
the neon-pale geraniums rappelling
on burgher curtains drilled with light
at night and night
tobacco-stained by day, we lunge
made slow by the urge to love
untrammeled by the sirens'
aggrandizing thrust. A gaseous flame

leapt from the greengold filth of the canal,
the squatters' barricades lit up and their anointed faces
appeared in the journalistic probe
outlined in kohl like convict masks.
Unhinged from the mirage

and refuged on a park bench by the swans'
imperial sashay we splay
a fist across each other's back
and loaded with fact like methedrine
by the unvanquished halo from the *Terra
Incognita*'s strobe we hug.

To Draw the Warmth of Flesh
from Subtle Graphite

The architecture gives more comfort than the scenes
enacted in its armature, cream-quilted beds
divided by the skylight into squares
of sun and shade like alternate sensations
abandoned as by picnickers on shore.
How light the paper is

on which this all is drawn,
the ladder of old olive by the tub,
a recent innovation, buckles it with its gnarls.
The terrace door above sheds bars
of summer shadow through the rungs
and tiles the floor with diamonds.

We aren't there to mar the lazy arc
of light along its path from wall to trapdoor.
On the beach, where we might be, it's calm,
and also by the olivegroves and asters.
The terra-cotta tiles absorb the sun.
The village bell layers the air, birds, then an airplane

fly a line into the distant sea. The language
of the people there amid the smells
announcing dinner rises.

Between Two Seas

Tonight I think of Bouboulina,
the poetry she used against the Turks
to code intelligence in rhythm
from mountain to ravine to creek
and the subservient-looking peasants who worked there.
Only as strong as who came before us sings a tape

I use while working on my clients,
and I don't have the heart to edit it
though I dislike lyrics during bodywork
as too much enlisting the conditioned
mind in a direct communication between fields.
As I approach middle age, with the thrill,

more than unexpected, astonishing,
of having reached a mountain peak
after a decade's dawdling, accustomed so
to hoisting the self the stress
seems natural, and lifting
my eyes over the edge

in the resigned manner ascribed to maturity,
prepared to see the pinnacle then eke
another forty, human nature permit, inclined
downhill, only to stand before a broad
horizon-reaching mesa, full of brooks (in C major
for viola d'amore, the Greek

poet said), hills, valleys, blooms and all
the accoutrements of fauna a pastoral
metaphor can hold, an era broad, stable
and, in its upright stance, humane.

Endurance, serenity brought through
the blasphemous contradictions of an adolescence

to midthirty (until I lost all trace
of girlhood from my face, a friend said) clear
from heart to mind a threshing ground
where compassion, outrage, dignity
share breadth the sexual alone
had augured with its olive branch

let loose each time to fly.

She Loves

deep prolonged entry with the strong pink cock,
the sit-ups it evokes from her, arms fast
on the climbing invisible rope to the sky,
clasping and unclasping the cosmic lorus.

Inside, the long breaths of lung and cunt
swell the vocal cords and a rasp a song,
loud sudden overdrive into disintegrate,
spinal melt, video hologram in the belly.

Her tits are luminous and sway to the rhythm
and I grab them and exaggerate their orbs.
Shoulders above like loaves of heaven,
nutmeg-flecked, exuding light like violet diodes

closing circuit where the wall, its fuse box,
so stolidly stood. No room for fantasy.
We watch ourselves transform the past
with such disinterested fascination,

the only attitude that does not stall
the song by an outburst of consciousness
and still lets consciousness, loved and incurable
voyeur, peek in. I tap. I slap. I knee, thump, bellyroll.

Her song is hoarse and is taking me,
incoherent familiar path to that self we are all
cortical cells of. Every *o* in her body
beelines for her throat, locked on

a rising ski-lift up the mountain, no
grass, no mountaintop, no snow.
White belly folding, muscular as milk.
Pas de deux, pas de chat, spotlight

on the key of G, *clef du roman, tour de force* letting,
like the sunlight lets a sleeve worn against wind, go.

With God

In another life in a convent I
attending the aphrodyte
by constant dilation and distillation
of devotees
visitors or communicants
delighted alike
upslope the inverted bowl of the polis
where the omphalos spasm was felt to exist
a fault and throttle at the hearth
central to the foundation.

It pleased us
and god too to extract
from each adoration many
successive radiations
toward the sweet god bathing
in the eternal basin below
by our attention.

If I had said extract I'd have been tickled
and hot towels placed on my godly parts
funny rules
$\qquad$ I sweated it out

like waiting
for a smell to occur
as in early March
in the hardy bud
of the lavender fields
of our region.

No drawing back for fear of drawing
such pleasure away. Athletic.

Etymology

I understand her well because I too practice love
for a living. She came for therapy which I explained
from the root *create*, as in the cognate *poem*,
and *theros*, summer harvest and heat,
and how the ancient prostitutes, *therapaenidae*,
practiced the poetry of heat. She had
enjoyed the whoring but not the pimp
she railed against
so loud in our fourth session
I ducked to keep the pressure with my thumbs
and covered my ears with her breasts to bear her decibels.
"Red trails of poison up my thighs, goddamn him.
Beat on my head all day last time I saw him,
and when the cops arrived, *Her boyfriend*
beat her up. Stopped by to see if I could help.
He had the bad luck later to blow a cop.
Tooth and heart. Isn't everything?"
No. Faith as prelude and spine.
That is a more important.
That is a larger that.

Tryst

The human cunt, like the eye, dilates
with pleasure. And all by joy never named

now are priceless in the magnitude of the stars.
From are to are, have to have, beat sub-eternal.

By day, I found these on the beach, for you each
day and give. By night, remind me, I have

forgotten. Action replied by action, peace by peace.
Take you in all light and lull you on a sea

of flowers whose petals have mouths, mesmerized
centerfold, upsweep toward sleep.

For Every Heart

I like it when my friend has lovers, their happy moans,
unrestrained, fill the house with the glee of her prowess.
As in China, during the concert of the laser harp,
cameras added their applause, percussive,
while the umbilical fanned neon from each note
in the open-air theater and ribboned the path of stars,
I am moved to clap. Hands clapping calm us.
It is their simple, wholehearted and naive sexual imitation,
their fleshbird dance chest-high in the open of time.

Field

I had a lover. Let us say we were married, owned
a house, shared a car. The trees were larch, white birch,
maple, poplar and pine, the mountains granite,
and three months of the year verdantly lush. We met

cows, sheep and horses on our walks up or downhill
a fine dirt road. In time, my lover came to take
another lover, of whom I also became enamored.
There is a seagull floating backward in a rare

snowstorm on an Atlantic ocean bay as I remember this,
its head at an angle that suggests amusement.
This younger lover flew home to a far Southern state
and returned in a large car with several rare instruments

and a Great Dane, a very spirited animal who had to
be returned to a family estate in the Midwest soon thereafter,
having discovered and devoured a neighboring farmer's chickens.
The seagull flies laboriously into the wind

the length of my windows, then settles to be floated back.
It is a young bird, wings black-tipped and grey.
We added a room to the cabin that summer, the work done
by a young sculptor from the college, one who seemed

to be continuously counting, a devotional attitude
that appealed to me. One evening we returned to find
a note pinned to our door, Call Ted abt a possible free piano.
That it did not materialize did not affect my feelings

toward him and in September I moved my area into this room.
Fifteen by seventeen, it had a long wall of salvaged windows,
a door with a sturdy ladder to the forest floor,
a wall of the enormous cedar logs of the main cabin

and, to it, a soundproof door with a double window
Ted had devised. Our younger lover took over my old area,
and my lover continued working upstairs
where the rising heat of the Franklin caused her

to take off her clothes frequently, as well as open a window.
We bought a large futon for my room, and next to it
laid a smaller futon, what is called a yoga mat, turned
the quilts sideways and slept facing the luminous birches

in differing night lights. Enormous fireflies
when the temperature hovers at thirty near midnight,
early September, late June. Daylight was often a wrathful time,
and it is a tribute to the height of our spirits

that we barely noticed, gliding over it as we did
over friends and professions. The phenomenon of three hearts
dilating as if in unison, eyes diverging toward
each one, rare, blasted our systems with tremendous energy

and within the year we packed each a bag, compromised
on five instruments, of which two collapsible, and a small amp,
and flew to a continent where one of us knew one country's
language. We traveled, fought, separated and reunited

for six months, then were joined by an old friend, traveling
with whom we thought a lover, who turned out
a companion instead, a tall, stately model with the gait,
approaching us on the beach, of a sulky seven-year-old.

Our younger lover's age, they played music together,
and together got stranded in an inflatable boat
whose outboard motor they'd flooded. *I sacrifice
myself to the sea*, chants our lover, unforgettable

in this scene if unwitnessed, as the model struggles
with the four flimsy oars and, *Row, damn it!*
They made it to shore half a mile east of our house,
and were towed by a small speedboat belonging to a man

who had tried to fix their motor, he standing in
his fiberglass, they trailing behind, past the entire
village on their wooden chairs outside the grocery,
the eating house, the front garden doors. The model

was extremely cheerful at dinner, having hauled the canvas
tub to the yard, our lover wounded in pride and spiteful.
We lived in that house on the edge of the water
for two months, until our money ran out and we returned

to our wooded hill, our friend and companion to their town
by the eastern tip of a Finger Lake, seven hours by car
further inland. My lover and I found our jobs
during our leave had been embittered by our firm's

acquisition by a larger establishment affiliated with
the military. We resigned, or rather, refused the new
firm's offer, and shortly thereafter moved to my friend's
town where I accepted a federally funded position for

my skills in music and massage, a divergence
that delighted me. We rented a farm out of town, partly
on work exchange, feeding and caring for two horses,
two dogs, one of them slightly mad, six cats and a senile

bunny. This our lover agreed to do, as well as stacking
most of nine cords in a fit of jealousy every morning
of the week my lover was in California. They were actually
face cords, the pile would have measured four and a half

in our old county. They made a terrific racket,
hurled across the yard into the barn, where the dogs
from their pen greeted them. The farm was on a straight
north-south road, they couldn't be trusted loose

in the four-wheel-drive traffic, they were barn animals
and couldn't be kept in the house, but their barking
from their large, humane, indoor-out pen with running brook
and bales of hay had an ungrateful sound that made us

ignore the fence when they broke it, to the chagrin
and later vituperation of the owner who kept our deposit.
My lover returned from California with three bottles
of fine red, one of them a Petite Sirah, purple velour

tops for us, and the seedling of a new self profoundly
and coincidentally engendered by a brief affair with
the lover I'd left to move East to our cabin. Our younger
lover didn't recognize the smell under the fingernails

as I did, with pleasure. It is impossible to disengage
from jealousy someone told me in graduate school.
It challenged me to find a course that wouldn't feed it,
and have put my mind to it since, profiting only

from a general graciousness, nonchalance, fatality. The snowfall
that winter was heavy and the winds tore savagely to one side
of our four-mile road. By what should have been midspring
our lover had contrived to be collected to the faraway

Southern state and we did not care to pursue the deposit.
Though we were broke, a sensation like shutters beating
bodily in the stillness that followed the April storms
preoccupied us exclusively, though I did see the lilacs

crashing it seemed through the old barn walls,
and the hill go green on the stain of the bellyshot doe
before the snow. We moved, with my friend, to California
for a summer job arranged by my old lover, and we four

spent the season specifically amiably, in fairly rigid
pair formation, I and my friend – who had first become
my lover under my younger lover's hand while abroad by the sea,
a gesture delicate and precise, savored by all and regretted

bitterly and immediately by the youngest – my old lover and
my lover. We lived and worked, teaching nutrition, healing
and survival skills to young adults, in what had been a Navy
compound on a Pacific Coast beach and had long hours

of simple sitting, and staring. I brought my guitar
and practiced hearing in detail my picking against foghorns
and gulls. My lover sang. My friend was a little insecure
far from home, and clung, peacefully, to my middle.

In the fall we moved to be half the staff at the halfway
house here. The pay was low but secure and we each rented
a studio facing the bay for the off-season. We did not travel
together. Rather, my lover flew directly, my old lover

via the Midwest to visit family, and my friend and I
drove the car. *Snow Creek, Lake Crescent, Ruby Beach,*
Humptulips, Tokeland, Palix, Parpala, Hug Point, Arch
Cape, Perpetua, Darlingtonia, Bliss 14, Pacific Fruit

Express, Grace, Power County, Sweetwater, Harmony,
Adora, Amana, Homewood, Vermillion, Presque Isle.
We've lived here four months, a full holiday season,
friends from inland and the West. My lover and I

bicycle the dune roads to the ocean. The winter is mild,
and the bay home to seven varieties of duck that I've
sighted, and seagulls and pipers and pigeons that sit
on the railing to hear the guitar and are annoyed

PERPETUA

and shift and scold if I should lose my concentration
for their flattery. My friend and I cook meals for our
festivities, and make love for exquisite hours when I may
scream and contort myself but on leaving the house

remember nothing, no, not nothing exactly, I remember
if put to it, but not ordinarily. My old lover and I
are affectionate, my lover and I are cheery, and our
younger lover recovered and moved to a large city nearby

and infrequently visits my lover and lately, lightly, me.

Lying In

Morning.
Who never sang before is singing.

That open avenue, tree-limned,
by which is known a city
domed palatino to triumphant arch,
that fountained thoroughfare,
banked by the broad facades, bone-white,
of arcade shade in sun,
that splendid rectilinear
lay of center city, not wholly
squared but bowed as was
known to the Greeks, physical
marble memory of sheaved-
in-a-column trees, eternal
iconostasis whose noon
is twelve and midnight six o'clock,
hill-cradled basin
transfigured as by tiers
of balconies where linens
gently take the air
between their seams and pull
against the balustrades
to join the light, that
swath, that aqueduct become,
like the cherubim and seraphim
we must aspire to, nothing
but eye, view, opening
to light, that fairway
whose incarnations recollect
god unknown
and immanent as faith

feeding on our emotions,
that crown, that head
bone having moved
to the hilarious
wind of seed and blood
in sinuous symmetrical
rotation down the apse,
the apex of the body,
stairwell, *allea*, boulevard,
its split reveals
like Bashō's fish
the Buddha we have eaten.

The Way a Child Might Believe

I think now how we biked toward the sand
all day and up the hill at Devil's Elbow
in time to see a green ray, magma of the sun,
darken the dazzled rim of the Pacific.

We liked to feel the earth under our feet
turning as though our pedals made a difference,
as though it turned from Florence to Eugene
to kiss our wheels as we rode west to meet it,

sweaty and blissed. A borrowed bike at twenty-one
was like a Guggenheim. It rained. We laughed.
The sixty miles of woods have left a sound,
an imprint I return to in your image,

the way a childhood talismanic word
repeated will repeat the walls it echoed.
There are no walls. The day is green.
Green is the night, midfield on our returning,

cowed by the rain, asleep in our tube of tarp.
There is no who I was before that happened,
placeless and innocent, filled only
by a desire to have seen, have had

the carpet of stars infixed. As with your face.

Attitude

I let them whip and fuck me,
engaged in a passion I did not want them

to understand. They used a paddle and their hands
were large, their cocks youthful and pretty,

one red and shiny and very hot, one blithely
sheathed. They played about me, tying, untying,

vying the better posture or hold. After supper
they rubbed my clit and made me count backward

from a thousand perfectly, fingerfucking my ass
before they'd let me come. Bright windy afternoons

mid-spring and early summer, Tiger Balm on the clit
to keep it hot. We were strangers in town and,

as we were leaving soon, felt free to bring
others home from the bar to fuck me, showing off

how they sucked my nipples from the side
to make me tremble and wet. I never touched them,

and they would tickle and lick each other
in camaraderie or greed, impatient for their turn.

We went to the movies on other nights.

Days of Argument and Blossom

Energetic and long,
the way a dolphin's swim tickles the sea,
you play with me, both right and wrong, and softly

the turning fern fans your ass.
I used to rub myself with sand,
nostalgic for salty idiom. Offer me

the nude world of your back. The wind
overturns a glass of water. Or, you turn.
Your palm, your suntanned breast, the triangle

of your elbow.
Earth on a new eve, no lover,
no later that won't echo as refrain

our forty-five seconds out of orbit,
end of May among wind-twisted pine,
the roof and terrace tiles

a crimson game of solitaire
against the saffron shadowbox of moon,
the species a score for chord instrument,

daylight and eye, and the eye
not apologizing, knowing
its scope beyond the periphery

of night cast on the physical
world from its stained
glass membrane, the apex

of its dome. What *if* one memorized
the *Iliad* in school? Stubborn and generous
about our pleasure let us be as we,

unaccountably happy here,
escape the wait to hear the spit
fall on the scythe of hours.

PART III

for Susan

Lumens

There are no secrets
It's just we thought that they said dead
When they said bread

JOHN CAGE

OH LORD

I love when you take over
Her eyes and pierce me with your sky

THE KNIFE

Love of life
I promise to remember you

Each time we meet is the last

THE BIRD

To make poetry's possible
At home even briefly in the human wild

EACH LOVE

Parallel
Infinite
Unequal

NIRVANA STAIR

I come from small seas littered with
Playful islands

Feel how my heart is shaped
By that sheltering

CUSP

When you touched me
taking all that time
an ancient
and consecrated city
in orbit for centuries
found its dome

TATTOO

A child is a lonely thing to put in prison
Without a lover lonely in its parents' care

BRIDGE

A song unhinges bitterness easy enough from sorrow
Some vowel litany with stops to pass until
The most ordinary is not

AFTER YES

To build the chair
To build the chair
To build the chair
To sit
To sit
Witness the mystery
World

PRIVACY

Finally
    the only one I want
        to caress is you

You watch the changing
    light across the sky
        I watch your eyes

TEACUP

Flared at the lip like clematis
One swallow
Raised bottom where the sugar sleeps

FLORIDIAN

It's not just that you're wet but that you're swollen
Ocean where for me you dip

THE SEPARATION

Where desert boulders cleave: two stars
Small in the V, large up above

Where last I slept with you the tide
Eases the mark

DEVOTEE

I am grooming the body and rays of the sun
That will rise on the day you return

THE RETURN

As when setting a candle
In the molten wax of the one burnt low
In the hot candelabra

THE CROWNING

Baby, I call you, you
In me as if

INTERVAL

Two months since I sucked your nipple first
Eggplant purple then fig blue the taste
Drawn from your inner body lingers

CHASTE

Asleep
Mouth to mouth
For an hour

EVE TO GOD'S BACK

Leave me the snake
It is the you before the screen while you are gone

SELFISH

It's true musicians please
The public with their pleasure, but we
Eschew the stage

NIGHT AND LIGHT

Because your hand is my hand and my eye
And taste and smell and spirit I am I

THE PEACEFUL FIST

I said inside the small
Cathedral of my cunt eleven years before
That awning
Rose round the folded altar of your palm

As the seed of a mole for
Generations carried across
Time on a woman's belly
Flowers one morning blackly
Exposed to poison and poison
Itself is not
Disease but mutation is one
Understanding the strong
Shaft of your clitoris I kiss
As the exposed tip of your
Heart is another

The Choir

The Choir

I walk and I rest while the eyes of my dead
look through my own, inaudible
hosannas greet
the panorama charged serene
and almost ultraviolet with so much witness.
Holy the sea, the palpitating membrane
divided into dazzling fields and whaledark by the sun.
Holy the dark, pierced by late revelers and dawnbirds,
the garbage truck suspended in shy light,
the oystershell and crushed clam of the driveway,
the dahlia pressed like lotus on its open palm.
Holy the handmade and created side by side,
the sapphire of their marriage,
green flies and shit and condoms in the crabshell
rinsed by the buzzing tide.
Holy the light –
the poison ivy livid in its glare,
the gypsy moths festooning the pine barrens,
the mating monarch butterflies between the chic boutiques.
The mermaid's handprint on the artificial reef. Holy the we,
cast in the mermaid's image, smooth crotch of mystery and scale,
inscrutable until divulged by god
and sex into its gender, every touch
a secret intercourse with angels as we walk
proffered and taken. Their great wings
batter the air, our retinas bloom silver spots like beacons.
Better than silicone or graphite flesh absorbs
the shock of the divine crash-landing.
I roll my eyes back, skylights brushed by plumage of detail,
the unrehearsed and minuscule, the anecdotal midnight
themes of the carbon sea where we are joined:
zinnia, tomato, garlic wreaths
crowning the compost heap.

The Continuo

            Happenstance,
a storyline between the surf's
palindromistic shuttle,
it is your wind
tonguing our holes
until they sing your tune.
It wasn't something
we could have told you.
Background radiation
has been the paradigm for so long
and your communal
intuition pervasive invisible
grid. The potter
at least once holds the sky
in the forming cup. No one
drinks from another. Every palm
upturned invokes a stream,
the wisdom to sip the wind
coursing downhill for rot.
In its entirety
the song is owned
like a bottomless cup
set on the earth it opens
a small round hole to the other side:
sky, if it were only night
and we not asleep
on our antipodal.
But it is night
there and the star
we glimpse on a lucky alignment
is thought a sign
of aging in the chosen

eye. The strip of green
bamboo buffeted by a squall
at cove's edge sends its dry
laughter our way. And birds
in the early morning
loudly foretell.
Sleep fades like snow thrown on August's guitar.
You mark our brow like a great even keel
scraping the shale to shore
in the roofers' hammers
the tow-truck's diesel civet
the windsock's dizzy spin.

Offertory

Holy the untouched mothers
beating their shining girls.
Like passengers
in a speeding car
step on an absent brake, they break
into our spirits driven
to seizure unto death then calm
but dumb, our starving
deaf-mute relatives whose urgent
simulacrum meets
no equal eye.
Holy the streaming eye
of girls whose bones have broken
some household instrument awry
from its simple task: hair
to be brushed, clothes
hung, cloth
measured, food, god almighty,
waiting to be cut.
There is a native flowing
of love toward one's mother
and father if he's there.
What's broken in the beaten child
is the transparent channel
from its heart
to the punishing armor.
Holy the earthly afterlife
amid the sea of shards
offering the ungiven:
the woman casting
armloads of net behind her boat
at midday will not stop.

Even supine
on fields abud with chamomile
in northern Minnesota
under the moon's eclipse
we see her
traverse the penumbra in a blaze of light
from wet and muscled forearms.
She is blinded
in one eye and can bear
on her leather patch
the unmuted decibels.

Grace

Air
through which invisible birds are flying
conducted us.

You show me everything
not only what you know
if I quiet myself by unclanging
the obvious.

Sleeping poorly I have your skin
overnight a field expanding on the tongue
extinguishing the sentence.

The shape of your hands and feet
undefended has schooled me.

The dream of prayer your nightmare interrupts
takes days to rain its forgiving mantle
through our slow matter
yet was our sheet.

We wouldn't assist the hand that struck us.
We wouldn't eat garbage.
Words from the prison island
our childhood spine.

The Contemplation

You are home and the sound of your steps to the running water
in the deep porcelain bath lets me rest. In my quiet mind
your white body, slim as a blade of light, immerses and lifts.

In my quiet heart, in the late summer season, a word, like a
single boat on the sea's luminescence, at dusk. The boat
stirs the fireflies of the water, and the lone walker trails a

kite-tail of kelp, exciting the mystery. If you look from your
window, boat, footfalls, kelp, plash a comet of light on our
cooling beach. The window in your heart and in my heart opens

to face the world illumined by the shy word at its center.
They are two windows and two hearts and though they open on
the coastline of the endless world they have one frame, one

glass, like a sheet of the clearest gel secreted by the body.
A child, born of the word, walks through the sash offering its
small round hand touching everything, a blur of brief imprints

suffusing the blood. Such sudden whiteness in the cells of
the body like sleep overcome by gardenias. Like milk cooling
in the pail on the stone floor of an unused room through the

night. At breakfast it nourishes with unexplained sweetness,
and the pot of gurgling rice for the noonday meal, and the
steam of soup for the evening supper collect like halos.

The word feels round and we guess at its meanings, kissing
the air, surrounding the air with flesh, and the air, the
immortal soul, shapes our lungs in its image. Butterflies

circle us in their mating season, the common white and the
brilliant poppy, trailing bright copies of those hidden wings
up the winding road and the stone promontory, all the way to

the lighthouse at Point Beach.

Paper Flute

Shortest light
of the year I greet you

unfamiliar to the yield of this
large inhibition the wind

soughs equally through
tupelo and lung the sculpt

of a greater nakedness
in the bones.

By Whose Hand

As if we were two
separate bodies rising
on two separate breaths
we work on different levels

one even goes away
far while the other
enacts a spiral circling
of the house

the enabling tasks
are satisfying and outside
everywhere life contrives
endless varieties of parcels

each breathing water
air or light
even though we love
and are confused by appearance

walking home the cat
avoids the skunk
they are both so shiny
are the leaves

not the season
are the bedclothes
which you have straightened
not the root

of a dreamless interstice
the harness tenderly
rendered invisible
first then retrieved

Family

Music composed during a war
performed in occupation

everything we are fighting for
encoded in its arms

air inhaled in the fetterless
exhaled to fill the shelter

when they got out of solitary
for singing they sang the songs

they had practiced there
because the others were older

they were sixteen
a resuscitation like roses

from the barbwire canals
our mothers and fathers

Collaborations

T Begley and Olga Broumas

from

SAPPHO'S
GYMNASIUM

faithful the present I see you

Helen Groves

What if there were no sea
to take up the table of our hearts
breath which is everywhere curved
hand from infinity broken

Went walking and walking
far off to get water
two people with your birds
mirrors for multiplying light
we serve

Peaceful limbs
had been little breathless
branches of two humans
the gods are openmouthed

I saw her foot
then a church burning down
with its figure of water then star starkness
she is all I was dead but I was born again
head to guts in her blanket

Islandlike in the morning
she bathes in wet beaver creek

waiting for the sun to warm
limestone boulders dark lip

By long kiss the icon is
worn a lighter color
than the rest of the face
bathing the living

In the turning of the sun she is the shining path
faith tender muscle

It's not the herbs on my lips
we have freedom to be
infinite or not at all
infinite or not yet

I am optimistic I am scared a little
what really matters is realism now
incurable
too the environment produced from our feelings
my friend it is possible
to drink the ecstatic one's ecstasy
over the source of energy I drink it

Where I presently stand my heart can see
peacock overnight then morning quail
how long the sex on your fingers
even when the hand stopped breathing

I set my sailors east toward our island
took remains of a watermelon lunch
I ask her to help me out of my body
at end of hunger so few needs
wind flies ahead

Our day begins in preparation of the silence
the silence is us
daily I want nothing nothing but this dispatch

After barns and wild growing
along fern bank
pairs of young sparrow are hollow I sit in
plus your small loud stream whose birds
I may obtain forty days
mirror pure

I come single
alone
under my clothes

The summer without sheets the unclothed girl
a cloth of oxygen to sleep beneath
the innocent hills

Lush birding covered
the wood black and ringing
cedar blooms in migration
warblers on fat ridge

Immature adult
turned brilliant red
always you smell so good
in the bowl undividable sleep

Exits everywhere entrance touched your face
after multiple helpings my heart works perfectly
my head far overhead not far from the fantastic
deep sacred racing about
in the acre of fire makes vessel

Rake it stone by stone upthrusting
my ground to be that's what I dig
receiving skin amid unceasing

I don't know virgin
when I was made I was made

Quiet that has known us
from loneliness to quiet
bird heart know our bed
you with your light

Scare of separation our third day
blossoms small scar
easily covered

And the cure
ready
ready for you

do I mean
on your body
the wafer

Pod of whales in the heat
beautiful torsos nearby
I watered you

All night
under the blankets
fair peeking

Desert silence
who must constantly beat her wings

You'll like the worshipers
the sky with its seacoasts of Greece
what kind leaves home for home
send me

Vowel Imprint

Transitive body this fresco amen I mouth

Directly behind door are sandalwood hibiscus
birdhouses in the rain on open land
I make a new one using scrap
for us

Will these floors burst in oxygen
my life spent swimming
inside the cleanest house cleanest bed
sleep of envy probing the ranges of light
nutrients from side to side
infinity acquisitions

How can my body not be sorrow shoulders light
against lips held for hours
and hours the flute
cranes in their nests

You feel the bruising midflight as one born
to dazzle god with your own heat
beside me on the bed your foot
taken into my mouth
I tongue the injured core of its birthright
and the hot burning off of self which exhausts it

Sometimes I don't put away the tools
ripened in shade by the ruined house
with its own whiteness walking upland

neighbors stood and watched it
watched it some more
leafless trees bore shadow

darker in the pasture
the tops of our bodies were hard
ball of blood sent rolling and not shy

I like to be your digging stick
marital female mass

Arresting melancholy seeking to touch
slavery with medication
art calms

Where I unbind my hair light's first blue witness

Like flocks of solitudes surrender
a bird beautiful and uncovered
I bite small seas into your heart
populate with birds a sky
immaculate with shriek of wing
for its updraft I have married

I have procreated
unless writing
studies the image
and no more

I am not alone
facing the sun
lover of all

Flower Parry

Clear blue temple I'm taken in
clear blue temple I'm taken in
god would talk if I did
god would talk if I did

got a mouth wants to know

I was seeing someone burst open
I was seeing someone burst open
the door she was being
the door she was being fucked

hurt as a virtue

hurt as a virtue makes me
vertigo piss-scared
seeing someone burst open
god would talk if I did

Sophia I said I have been squatting
it is hot and wild in here amassing the mysteries
let go your hammering
I can aim in any direction and miss
and miss every time
with effort
I can miss with effort
back of my hand
back of my head
no matter how painful
dancing in your mirror

because it is my mirror
if it came from my heart

Walked toward the garden
I had work to show it
then I understood the garden was destroying it
and that I should rest and not water the
shoots in the dark but wait until dark to
uncover them

Rich red euphoriant pumped by heat
at high magnification
in the lightest scan
sweat kicking dense now
the indescribable screams of the ego cleansing

You who are being titillated go
thrive on the tiled plaza to the sea
don't breathe our air into the dark
anti-lips eyes tongue
how come you play for maggots
when juice of air itself gives law
touch my throat I will shatter
god with restraints I'm not

Incest animal
you stop to give me a ride
grace is rendering
my old self unchanged

oppressing witness by innocence
birdsong in fist undressing

Passed on by kicks its name is bad
bad doors and windows do its work
court after who courts after
I am more stupid where it strives
first it then me the power of the cage
tamper spoil and lose its asp
split breastbone that was my life
on panic

Pour down avalanche of palms
someone's pulses aim to do as soon as possible
lightening the feet dressing the lips
tenderfoot seedbed in the spirit given rights
over vast agreement

Praising floor carried into fields a synonym of life

Practitioner without practice asylumed by her side
at first death and afterlife or even contact craving
frightened me but in commonlight at the lamphole
angel eyebright charge of dreams
shaking the vulgar tablecloth each of us
her splendid gaze mantle burning

I don't know why I serve or want to dance wake up be born
watching the window settle on compassion
molecules learned healing people came to drink
I made a wing which we are flying
mountain covered with saints
nice of them to leave the baskets
no moral life is without
individual years creating embrace
how easily it could has changed one bit
I do myself o solitude
at the birthing of sea level
my undesired you ask undestroyed

Resting is possible
whose shock fills my mind
past once then the real

Birth becomes familiar
I spit on the rocking wings
it's like nothing
I say to myself
foreign spell
I say to myself
shoving my legs inside
these warm wounds

Never metaphoric
same tiny hole someone has seen
and has remained
to admit it
I was born easily at home
broken habit of mother
I weep
that is all

Your Sacred Idiot with Me

Sitting in a rowboat
not rowing
investigating you

After the roots have spoken
your night cries

Look after me true
true wherever

A soul I did insist upon
I live superimposed

Without a hint of choking
without hesitation
ethical in our nerves
hugging and squeezing
a brain that keeps
ejaculating molecules
in the visible
time poets shine

Came to earth just earth and nothing else
then spirit was born clear easy guest
equal during exposure second

Wonderful mineral like lemon being eaten
in my gums filled with saliva
your translated trance I am performing it
asylum through my clearest my solid birthright singing
full time mercy break god

Joinery

Long my heart has been
home you feel the most
my arms will tell

Unconscious pocket like new grass
in time of war
you dig one hole I fit rock

I didn't cover myself
I looked instead right back

Art is climax over conduct
Zen of no color by sunrise I do

Here at the threshold we took off our cloths
and though I don't remember everything I remember the place
I first saw death seeking a wound and since then one other
sensually nothing I can by now recognize an injection of sleep
spinning clobbered with substance
willing to be sung

I stand in the dark
like photography beaming
the fruit measures itself

asking with my hands
yet more explicit
word with god

Small garden greatest garden I write out
your passions though what I noticed was a jolt
once again this idea I enjoy forgiving

High sky I fell and I forgot cover our tent
you know you shade me
shovelful of pebbles getting lighter at the bedside
losing my hospital vocabulary because just
my everyday fear you hold by the stem

Our maker's void I silence boulder why do you quake
light over here moves her hand
roadkill like myself
massive daylight in the grave mass grave

Cure for water is water
one very blue throughout the trees
divine indulgence yesterday
the cross dove from the wall
naked cross get into lifeboat
reincarnation or not

Antennae in the shale with big
microphones jacked in our jewels
remote from sensing eye in sky
human kindness there's a light
drifted far out I can help it
echolocate

I'm done reading your book and admiring you
grape-sized obedience
scaffold with force like sandblast
inside and out minderror mirror
I was silly finding good
your idea

The scary thing gets nervous when I lift it
I spent enough on that
kid harness well-oiled
on the lawn spread gravel
for the skinless with salt

Fondest maker I wake up in the dark
hoarding one craving speech
stay married sees divinity deliver

Fast asleep on the sleeping bed
particularity could do no more
columns curled upon the quiet
serving at her throat

On faith from some artist's image
a sheet of paper saying you are possible
I thank the artist for that
island continent its small aborigines
values I stand on I invent
and in the very middle of that gap
the givers

Digestibles of Sun

Don't ever cut me from your hands
take all your drink from me
dry lips from the turning kiss my own
fleece from the flock as one true compass
to bear the overpowering morsel
never goes off

Give me your hand candidate for the light
the light won't wake you
nor the fragrant wetting just begun
to join the litany of the visible
we go in
and out of the lung

My thinking is play
my writing is play
child don't change species when it know
the physical properties of rainbow

Language you surge
language you try me
I set a place for you
who would have guessed there were so many
similars you with your light
plotted across my window
we are walking toward it arm around
shoulder what else

Because I am preparing
because it is not possible
you bruised me making the indelible erosion
in the blood part seas part cries
as a body sixty-two days of no rain
found its way to life
from the waist down one nightwinter
slips a hand into the clay and digger

Burnt both hands waiting for you
still unwashed
sheet scent let it be my hands
leading you

May you always sing in the way of paint
of which many are vowels as well as colors
rest and be truth in sound and play
be its phonographer
for its own sake for poetry
find again what you have known with
a deer's small pelvis fostering range
as field is cream of a long river

Mistaker repeat the mistake
ignore my close attention be
blind to the silence of eyes

I heeded your great activity
every sinew every point all
the firings little grey
panels of light I heeded you

Who's watching my heart
earth expected many
of the one in my temple
with the steel short hammer and the flare

I dare take you up again
three-quarters of every day in the irrepressible acre

Stunned a crimson flower sudden
but not surprising the sunny addiction
the barely possible thirst

Sprig then when stronger leaf
I lie all night with her
I live where she is many
committing cleanness
the chosen chemical suffusing the harm
to the end of helping city
I'm on the side of I spread myself around

I look forward to it
I get on my knees

On the way to clearest practice the one I want
        takes my offering
unaided rose outside the chapel
gigantic in the unfurled song
under her feet the prows
of boats in the stilltide

I dream in the land
I lose all sensation
I last an instant
dazzling altar
angels and angels
one church

Insomniac of a Zen-Garden Fruit

Mortal in things I want to pray with you
sleep that rests face to face
so few sympathetics
untroubled by modesty or shame feel your pearled
halo from dreaming sleep that rests

Amber on hills the day begins
the light upon me a kind of body
whose bird it is the very blue
mercy accord to slave

Feel at ease sitting at our side
if you say bloody arm then bloody arm
if you say wheelchair then wheelchair
never move from what you tell

I'm setting down my open hand
drugless birth without a code
watching her drink milk
my marriage

Photovoltaic

Lord let me all I can wild cherry
I'm dazed all my ways of arriving bear tracks
failure of being torn to pieces is me
mumbling anxiety and I love my heart
I do each day lightly suffering desire
for kindness vividly today
idiot red unselfish green blue threadbare of cloud
outside the labyrinth imagining my life

Write poems
starve off death

Isn't the earth warm
the dew stars and the whole
yours for more work perhaps
inside we change work changes

Lord the voice was large
lord the voice is large
begging even

Nurse openly and everywhere
earth hand into being
you build
we care
you cut
we perish

tearing cloth apart
you are our tusk

I had no other dream
I reported back
for this large meaning
bent this way that vernacular with me
Eden after melancholy
palms suddenly heralds

Insistent love I won't outlive the words I lamb in your mouth
anachrist of the bewildered touch of extreme hands

Empty of shit the race is on
empty of eyes made of wood with indifference
don't you straighten it
don't pretend your mouth is not on fire
that stupidity bursts the needle
absolutely on the solid floor
race for the oar light sleeps to dream
travel through shining the ration before you
for every hurt be my large palm
Poetry

Sappho's Gymnasium

Outside memory worship never dies

That wish to embrace the great poplar

I woke and my head was gleaming

Trees fill my heart

Torn mist doves I will love

Light struts cannot be broken

Make praise populations will last

"I have a young girl good as blossoming gold
her ephemeral face I have formed of a key
dearer than skylark homelands"

A full twelve hours like a toiler like Lorca
archaic to bone we parse lark grove

Dutyfree dove seapitched Eléni
nectar your carafe seafounder

Preumbilical eros preclassical brain

Her face could still last tone of swaying habit
as if by accident the sea
exactly

Spasm my brakes
downhill oaks
eros wind

Beacon praise
hourless night
poet-taken

Lesmonia, Lemonanthis, Lesaromas, Lesvaia

Bird is drunk inside me
remembering the smell
at your door

You are the guest
heart traces

Out loud you fill
that doesn't exist

Justice missed hyperventilates poet
Buddha vowel in Mohammed child dared cross
far from mother olivegroves father almonds
lyric sap of maple far from Lésvos

The soul has a knee
just risen just rinses

Laurel to air I speak your lips
lantern in the abyss

I am what astonishment can bear
tongue I owe you

Pupil only to you
fleece of dew

Owl to her narrow-hipped tunic bread to her athlete sleep

Small iconostasis clay girls
recombine danger and Homer

Dearest on the unrolled robe
young wife with peace in her hair

In the dark before the candle
where the archetypes take our unconscious to build
this work is forever

Wanderer gathers dusk in mountains
to its end the wind the stream
only riverbank hurry me

Only poetry

ITHACA:
LITTLE SUMMER
IN WINTER

Pity lifts from me. I touch my cheek while everyone sleeps, the terrace is endless. I touch my cheek with your hand, grape split by the season our mouth. Help us in every way. Let our children live. Those the sea tires meander a greater ocean. It is dry there and a snuffled exegesis finds a coast in a shell. Let us turn into water. Baby eggplant mothered by oil. Yard herbs and those salty ones the boulder steeps. I am making you a spirit.

Your eyes at the end of seven days. Cold breath after sun, and with sun, the elixirs. On the way back they pull up young birches and bring them to the house. They say we are different, I say, toward each other the planetary eddies. Three birches, taken with their roots, are called pillars. Your eyes set them on the perimeter, soon we enter. The roots are awake and thankful, in the original soil and on our virtual stand. As they climb they become ecstatic. Utopian, unlike exiles, nested birds on the wing.

Blue sky, look at them they are walking over the mirror. I hold my word, scooping her in my arms. I climb the lip of the god. The vowel spirits walk my body. A dog was sitting there looking far off. We stand where nothing mirrors. From a distance the mouth seems hewn into delicate options. On it, I adore the dust. Whatever thought she follows, we follow too. Her tongue is the sea and all that rises beneath the upper firmaments creates our air. At any time we are found there, standing.

The slight camouflage of cheek reminds me of our vow. Seamless the frailest limbs stroke the length of our empty floor. From their graphs we distinguish her offerings. But the tree draws them fiercely, they adorn it, tempo slower and magnified for the eye.

I cannot lift myself to that precious shelf. When I am troubled I lift a rock from the mud and it is my mind. Cold water is dripping on the ground and she is turning it to us. I lift a rock from my soul. I put it on a shelf and wherever I go my eye rests on it. If I am very quiet while I shout to the multitudes, I do not forget. When I become the smooth rock, the rock to grind corn, the rock fitting palm, I am with you and we are the grains of dust on her lower lip. *Mer* of vowels. With you, the small temple at the corner of the room, far above the water.

I've the love of a sun house put up in the evening pine. The floor is bleached clean and the canopy a miracle to thermals. Somebody sees me and I was just looking at the ground. Alone the slip of wind restores her dressing. Scene of chaos quickens the outer globe. Slats, harmonious rolling orbs, climb onto my back. Let us make this hide.

Once, I had straps across my back. Some said sundress, some yoke. Modesty shelters. While riding the escalator, while scrubbing, while ministering, while holding your temper this side of smash, while failing to conquer. Stand with me on that lip. We have seen it crumble the parliaments. Be careful, be careful on the journey to heaven.

Caregiver to joy and hounds.

While you are walking, my mind changes. Windows the orphans open to sail kites, helium-tailed, crest our simple eyes. In countries where the light goes on longer and longer, whose color changes the slower we walk, medicinal pace, hieratic the humble. I walk behind you in my padded coat, between the elements, singing. I walk behind you in sleep, explorer of the forms and concentration and the mind. You let down the little bottle wrapped with a garment you wove with string. God is of us in the outer lining.

A large stone under which we pitched our scarves and gloves and ran ahead bare in winter now is the Buddha's footstool, the granite slab's omen, the palm's rest as we climb the stair. Stars are stones pitched by fire. Those we bring home from the beach, breasts of gods, help the corners we place them on keep flying. Sea-flag, sea-banner, sea-kite, sea-windsock, sea-butterfly and sea-net – so many places for the mind to snag its habitual and the body to gleam the righteous backdrop of joy's sweat, its rivulets, sunny arroyos flashing in flood. The shape of all shapes living together. Chaser see into me.

Cyclamen on winter table, sweeping the wood floor. We follow the ray of sunlight from its angles among the windowpanes, chart it with pallets, anchor it, a dial adorned with mammals, we say angel, or spirit, or cherub, meaning the light just glistened on the hair that fell from your dear scalp. Sheets sweep the day from the windowsill and the rooms are stripped clean as the lengthened beach where a rake made of stars and their diamonds patterns the powder finish of dreamers and the paralyzed outline of wills.

Direct belief is her elaboration. A field of poppies summers itself. Who loves underwater, who loves between columns of light and wind, persuades. Gratitude is the electron, I began to take care with my work of second winds. The mountains grow or fade through the tidal pattern, plucking out anger's teeth.

I have reached the pool at the end of the eddy and I hear your whispers again, and you take the cup into the sloping where it augurs more, and the mist of your breath is a finger that points the graze of god on my upper spine behind what was never bruised where the cemetery is just that, a place for sleep from which we awake.

Always I make inside your silence hair for the head of the poet.

Where we stood air stilled a standing cave. Quiet served us battening the angers from behind and her lateral muscles winged east and west, we were full-grown birds when she held us. Contours of rapture regress us, binary flight whose shades wander. I said urn you said peace I said nothing. Interior lightning made a heart. Peace returned my head.

I was taken apart under the green Moebius that held lightly the world's concussion. Untold cleanliness I admit you. Continue to take away nothing. My will is bent on feel recovered. She pulled me out who causes the sky to rise. This part is the vessel. Clay from the lower mountain statues its peak. We are the robes raking thyme and rosemary and the dust uphill. I am no longer embarrassed. Mild trees fruit their summer swallows, milky shade we absorb, appled sleep, amphora of raised arms.

Antiservitude on her street, and maples. Small numen her brow fills, outline of glass and poetry for human Alexanders.

Doves belong strictly for beauty a single can trigger. Respond heretically. A strange ivory made all things.

Her practice is water, her daydream is water. On the way to the wash plenty loves me. Milkcoat in the path releases her foot. Paradise is practice. Loosely woven, small in this bamboo basin, without blueprints the movement with the wind off the Orient and the movement upwards. Silence supports her.

The form of trees, like all teaching, is art. Exactly one is ringing without shame, and that tranquility rings itself into the heart of the mountains. The mind is whatever it is. Penniless and precious human life in another's help. Forget practice. Become exhausted. Can't practice. Delight me to live today by not flinching. Each day, over my past, I will help.

Busy in every room light has not yet reached, milk hush whose infant bindings have been loosened, proof sweeps the air. I take the meditation pillow to the kneecaps of a girl I love. Bird cleaning the cerebellum, the uninjured kites. WITH is occupation.

Moment the dead stop flying, flammable ego in the roar of lights, to be you survives me.

LARK

Praise praise as fast is lasting
immense double dare the unspeakable pulp
toe soiled
whose century I came to seek
its downstroke is the onomatopoeic world
I can't say weigh it
in its medium of honey I cross the sea
that bites and trains the burning teeth
on my eyelid

Abrupt loss lost
these are the signals beyond boredom
schoolyard water in the wilderness
milk in a room full of brooks

Kin to you are mantle nights
surplus hours sent from risk
night for hiding the goat
jolts for undamming bodies

Bearer of eyelight
bread kept clean
into the hands a few words stealing
knees from the fields of rainbows
stay empty my grief

Wind that has never passed through coined metal
Hour of staying I speak your lips

PHOTO
GENIC

Tha-Natos!

IOULÍTA HELIOPOULOU

Photo Genic

I am single and i am just

Gods touch me

I stand in the window a long time

No one closes it

Mother breaks the geraniums all day

Then she sets them in water

Under their table it's night

Only god touches me

I don't move but i'm swimming

I am invisible by the empty sill

Where god's sunlight adores me

Mother undresses my shadow

Its arms are long

Then its legs leave my feet and follow

I stand in god's arms forever

She shuts the door to my bedroom

I crawl out the window

July

NOTES

CARITAS

Caritas is the Latin root of the English words care, charity, charisma, and cherish.

BEGINNING WITH O

The poems in the first section, "Twelve Aspects of God," are part of a two-media piece that painter Sandra McKee and I worked on during 1975. It consists of a group of twelve oils of preclassical Greek gods, accompanied by twelve poems. The paintings were completed first and each poem grew out of the specific imagery of its painting, as well as the general significance of the myth. We tried, by using local women in contemporary dress as models, and by using contemporary verbal/visual imagery corresponding to the ancient myths, to express the continuity of those myths, and of female power, through the centuries to our own time. Our information on the specifics, significance, origins, and variations of the myths came primarily from Robert Graves's *The Greek Myths* and *The White Goddess*, and Elizabeth Gould Davis's *The First Sex*.

The paintings and poems were exhibited in September 1975 at the Maude Kerns Gallery, Eugene, Oregon, accompanied at the opening by a reading of the poems. In the spring of 1976, Lane Community College made a three-part presentation of the piece on its educational TV channel.

"Triple Muse"
The Muse was originally one, then split into three, and later nine, as the arts proliferated. Mount Helicon, the spiral mountain, was their home. Hesiod reports that they could make any falsehood believable through the elegance of meter and form.

"Io"
A moon god, often assuming the body of a white cow. She is said to have guarded the secrets of an alphabet closely linked to the lunar calendar and its phases. Because of her chosen totem animal, the cow, she has been described as slow-moving, gentle, and sensuous.

"Thetis"
God of the sea. She was attended by a college of fifty water nymphs, the

Nereids, and, controlling waters and tidal flow, was also believed to have powers over fertility, impregnation, and birth control.

"Dactyls"

Five gods that sprang from the imprint of Gaea's left hand on a muddy bank, one for each finger. They were closely linked to the earth, their mother, had oracular powers, especially through palmistry, and lived in sacred groves of Oak. They are believed to be the precursors of the Dryads.

"Aphrodite"

Originally god of midsummer and death-in-life, she annually destroyed the nominal King in an orgiastic ritual, as the Queen Bee destroys the drone: by mating with him and tearing out his sexual organs. In later years, her male priests practiced ecstatic self-castration.

"Calypso"

A demigod, possessing the power to grant immortality. She lived on an Ionian island, and is said to have been a painter, a weaver, and an accomplished storyteller.

"Artemis"

Well-known as the Virgin Hunter. Virginity, well into Christian times, signified absence of matrimony, not chastity. Her silver bow was a symbol of the new moon. The goat was sacred to her.

"memory piece / for Baby Jane"

I am indebted to Charles Wright for the word "lumescent," from his poem "Congenital," in *Hard Freight*.

"Bitterness"

The epigraph appears in the middle of a page of notes on Sappho. I have been unable to locate it in any of her works. It is possible that I wrote it myself, under her influence, or that it might be from some lyric in the *Greek Anthology*, though here again my efforts to locate it have been unfruitful. At the risk of mysticism, I feel the couplet to be hers, regardless of its actual provenance.

PASTORAL JAZZ

"Body and Soul"
Eleutheria: Liberty, common Greek female name.

"Sea Change"
Antonin: Antonin Artaud.

to move without embarrassment, / execute gestures without shame. – Mark Rothko.

A huge red arabesque derived from billboards and *A grid of many colors, like the underside of an old rug, / light and filmy, remains* – Lucy Lippard.

Rozan is famous for its misty, rainy days, / and the great river Sekko for its tide, coming and going. / That is all. / That is all but it is splendid. – from *Zen Mind, Beginner's Mind*, Shunryu Suzuki.

raw carrots, lettuce, radishes, olives and other things – Béla Bartók.

"Mosaic"
Title and form from "Psalm and Mosaic for a Spring in Athens" by Odysseas Elytis.

"Charisma"
After reading a work-in-progress by Lewis Hyde on gift economy.

"Jewel Lotus Harp"
And an artist an artist has to do what is really exciting – Gertrude Stein.

Beds we made of sweetgrass and magnolia / Petals – Pamela Powel.

To reunite the infinite with faith and *Bread to me is that velvet bud* – Eugenio Montale, translated by Charles Wright.

Articulation… quotation: assemblage of notes from the prose of Roland Barthes.

Four minutes 33 seconds: title of a composition by John Cage, consisting of rests.

NOTES

357

MOON

Written for the anthology *Beneath a Single Moon*, Shambhala Publications, 1991, edited by Kent Johnson and Craig Paulenich.

PERPETUA

"No Harm Shall Come"

Sophie: Sophie's Choice, novel by William Styron and film starring Meryl Streep based on the Nazi practice of asking a mother, newly arrived at a camp, to choose one among her children to accompany her, while the others were shot.

"After Lunch"

PX wives: Wives of American military and diplomatic personnel abroad who are entitled to shop at Post Exchange (PX) stores stocked with American goods. My mother worked as a clerk in the Athens store for several years, to secure the cost of my eye operation, but was not allowed to make purchases.

"Périsprit" and "On Earth"

Because Greece is so small and has been so densely populated over many centuries, there is not enough cemetery space, especially in the cities. This has given rise to the practice of burying the dead for four to five years, until only the bones remain, then excavating the bones and placing them in small metal lockers stored in mausoleums. Rarely, on unearthing, the melting, as it is called, is not complete, and the remains must be reburied for a time. Though I was extremely agitated and apprehensive about witnessing my father's exhumation, the actual experience was one of relief and joy to have him back on earth and in light with us again.

dancer... leading his circle of men: My father was an officer of the Greek army and on national holidays, dressed in a *tsolias* uniform of white, thickly pleated kilt, red tufted shoes, red fitted jacket with medals and braid, red fez and sword, led his command in the circular dances of our people. While the rest of the dancers perform sober, rhythmic steps, the leader, supported by the second dancer, leaps and twirls, striking his heels and forehead in the air, and the ground upon his swift return.

"Parity"

olive oil flung with sand: Technique used for shallow-water fishing at night. A rowboat is pulled gently through the water while a strong light shines from the prow to illumine octopi and squid. Handfuls of sand moistened with olive oil are flung as the boat advances, which clarifies the water and improves visibility and aim.

"Eros"

Vrijheid: Dutch word signifying freedom and love, antonym of apartheid.

"The Massacre"

Xerxes: Persian king of the late fifth century B.C. who, unable to cross the Bosporus on his way to war with Greece because of high seas, ordered his men to whip the waters. This act was always presented to us in school as ridiculous, though I see now that perhaps it allowed his army to vent its frustration and persevere.

The couplet *moonlight bright... read and write* is a free adaptation of the song Greek children would sing while walking at night to secret schools in churches or cemeteries during the Ottoman occupation of Greece from the thirteenth century to the mid-1800s. The teaching, and at times the speaking, of Greek was forbidden.

The gatherers of children: The Turks would routinely round up young male children from the villages and raise them in elite military camps. These young men, who then fought against Greek insurgence, were known as *yenitsari*.

Women would rather jump: This phenomenon was common enough to generate its own dance in several regions.

I am indebted, once again, to Charles Wright for the poem's motif "If I were..., which I am, if I were..., which I am," which has stayed in me for nearly twenty years.

"After *The Little Mariner*"

I had this dream the night I completed the last draft of the translation of Odysseas Elytis's book of poems, *The Little Mariner*.

"Between Two Seas"

Bouboulina: Young woman from Peloponesos, instrumental in the successful revolt against the Turkish occupation of Greece. As an adolescent I lived on a street in Athens bearing her name, behind the National Museum.

"She Loves"

Iorus: Umbilical cord

"Etymology"

"Therapy" breaks down etymologically into *theros* (summer/harvest) and *poio* (create). The Greek word for poet is synonymous with creator, as in the Greek Orthodox credo: "I believe in one God, father almighty, poet of sky and earth…"

"For Every Heart"

concert of the laser harp: Concert given in China by Jean-Michel Jarre on a harp of which each string released differently colored laser beams into the night when struck. On live recordings you can hear the clicking of cameras, like night insects, all through the performance.

"Lying In"

sheaved-in-a-column trees: It is theorized that the fluting of classical Greek columns is a visual remnant from the days when columns were constructed of thin trunks of trees bound together.

Iconostasis: screenlike stand for icons, usually between the bema and the nave in Orthodox churches.

COLLABORATIONS: SAPPHO'S GYMNASIUM

"Helen Groves"

Our day begins in preparation of the silence / the silence is us – Roland Barthes.

We began collaborating in 1983 when the American, new to Provincetown from classical Greek studies at Yale, asked the Greek to read a

passage of Aeschylus into a tape recorder for her pleasure and under-
standing. The latter was amusingly quelled by the contrast between T's
Erasmian pronunciation of Greek vowels and Olga's modern Greek, as
taught in the Greek gymnasium and later lyceum, but pleasure remained
in cadence and embodied emotion. "The wind of life hits you before its
material body, as the aroma of a woman before her actual presence.
What remains is the embrace, and love" – Odysseas Elytis. Syntax
swooped and leaned. Congas, saxophone, piano stood by.

Soon we began improvising in their syntax, and others we were to in-
vent or be invented by over the years, including sculpture (in schistolith,
metal, and epoxy), video, photography, installation, and performance art.
Syntax, the choreography of interval, dimension, tempo, and mood was
and is our primary medium, happily fertilized by snatches of Indonesian,
Latin, German, the Romance languages, Old English, pentatonics,
twelve-tone and Mixolydian scales, the microtonals of Asia, African
drum complexities abstracted in rock, chance, and divinized operations.

We have a poet's passion for this smattering of knowledges, eroticized
by suggested punctualities or ellipses, verbs in a variable middle voice,
nouns followed by their adjectives (imagine the object, then color it),
time divided into units other than Western certitudes. A tense for faith?
A tense for dream and trance? A semiotics of generosity? We practice
meditation in many forms. Who speaks? *Metis, Outis.* But, who speaks? A
voice of pluracination, heard partially, as always, gracing one of us with
particulars, the other with the hallucinated breath of verbally unintelli-
gible but musically incontrovertible dictions. That was one time, which
recurs. Another is certitude of the field it requires us to serve – eros:
gracious, philoxenous, augmenting, lubricant, remorseless faith.

We dwell, like most, in the lugubrious, cacophonous chaos of the im-
perial globe absorbed in its Babel complex. We don't have to sing about it.
"We wouldn't assist the hand that struck us. We wouldn't eat garbage,"
says Plousia L. of the rules conscience imposed on her and her camp-
mates for their survival during and after the Second World War. "That
which disempowers you is unfit for your song" – Odysseas Elytis. The
lyric refuses its raptor. Sappho's legacy to her daughter Kleis, her *gym-
nasium*, is "Tears unbecome the house of poets." This translation honors
her lithe tongue, if not the exact plurality of her meaning. The word for
"tears" is *thrēn'*, a contraction of *thrēnoi* (as in threnody), which is ono-
matopoeic and doesn't immediately imply words (why *ode* is needed in

threnody). It is the sonoric and somatic act of lamentations. For "unbe-come" she uses *ou Themis*, "not Themis," the female god of Justice and Ethics.

In Sappho's time the primary gods were female, *from your mouth to god's ear* an umbilical whose native wealth and dignity we never tire of guessing. Performance as the origin and culmination of text. What occurs in the simple swap is pleasure. Pleasure is infant, it too saves noth-ing. I mean the now that would have us undergo a surgery wherein "all light" is the only possible and desirable transplant. "Few know the emo-tional superlative is formed of light, not force" – Sappho's island-mate through millennia, Odysseas Elytis. My skin is the volunteer cipher of your emotion. I need a wafer, equal in body and propulsion, that devel-ops an entirely immaculate congregation of the tongue so that we might address you in words your love shapes.

Who speaks? The first draft of *Sappho's Gymnasium* consumed six reams of an intensely orange paper we had found for pennies. It stands a ragged tower in the towel closet, robe-colored, Buddhist. Collabora-tion is compassion. Erasure of "ego" and "muse."

> – *Written for* Dwelling in Possibility: Women Poets and Critics on Poetry, *Cornell University Press, 1997, edited by Yopie Prins and Maeera Shreiber.*

PHOTO GENIC

"Tha-Natos"

The last quote from a poem by Ioulíta Heliopoulou, from her book *EYXHN OΔYΣΣEI*. The title means "Wish/Blessing Towards Odyss-eas." The quote is a line break on the word "Thanatos," which separates it into the particle *Tha*, indicative of future tense, and the word *Natos!*, the Greek equivalent of "le voilà!", a semantic tour de force that has left me speechless since I read it.

ABOUT THE AUTHOR

Olga Broumas was born and raised in Greece. Her first book, *ANHΣYXIES*, was published in Athens in 1967 by Alvin Redman Hellas.

She came to the United States in 1967 through a Fulbright exchange program to study Architecture and Modern Dance at the University of Pennsylvania, and subsequently went to the University of Oregon where she completed an MFA in Creative Writing, with a minor in Dance and Printmaking. She won the Yale Younger Poets Award in 1977, the first non-native speaker of English to be so distinguished.

Her interest in dance led her to begin a lifelong study and practice of meditation, movement, and bodywork healing techniques. She became a licensed bodywork therapist in 1982 and has since used these skills in conjunction with the teaching of poetry and creative arts.

She has received Guggenheim, NEA, Witter Bynner, and State Arts Fellowships, and has published seven major collections of poetry and four books of translations from the Greek of Nobel laureate Odysseas Elytis, including the recent *Eros, Eros, Eros: Selected and Last Poems* (Copper Canyon Press, 1998).

She is currently Poet-in-Residence at Brandeis University and Director of their Creative Writing Program.

The Chinese character for poetry (*shih*) combines "word" and "temple." It also serves as raison d'être for Copper Canyon Press.

Founded in 1972, Copper Canyon publishes extraordinary work – from Nobel laureates to emerging poets – and strives to maintain the highest standards of design, manufacture, marketing, and distribution. Our commitment is nurtured and sustained by the community of readers, writers, booksellers, librarians, teachers, students – everyone who shares the conviction that poetry clarifies and deepens social and spiritual awareness.

Great books depend on great presses. Publication of great poetry is especially dependent on the informed appreciation and generous patronage of readers. By becoming a Friend of Copper Canyon Press you can secure the future – and the legacy – of one of the finest independent publishers in America.

For information and catalogs

COPPER CANYON PRESS
Post Office Box 271
Port Townsend, Washington 98368
360/385-4925
coppercanyon@olympus.net
www.ccpress.org

ABOUT THE COVER PHOTO

The image was created by Mark Power in 1980 at the Folger Shakespeare Library. Mr. Power had envisioned several sequences of time-exposure face studies, each concentrating on a profession or trade. He mentioned, to begin with, plumbers and poets. He wanted to see what might be revealed about each trade, and about each individual within it, by this method, which required the subject to be still for one to three minutes before the camera. He then envisioned showing these sequences in large format, perhaps applied to columns – the image I retained was very archaic. He spoke of "life-masks, how our face reflects the inward self when we close our eyes…" Apparently, after the first four portraits, he found a dearth of subjects "willing to suffer the daunting technical requirements…" I have been fortunate to have had an artist's proof of his eye on me for the last twenty years, and am very grateful to him for it, for his vision, and for his kind permission to reproduce it on the cover. – *Olga Broumas*

The typeface is Janson Text, created while Hungarian traveling scholar Miklós Kis worked in Anton Janson's Amsterdam workshop in the 1680s. The design inspired revivals by both Mergenthaler and Lanston Monotype in the 1930s. Adrian Frutiger and others at Linotype contributed to this 1985 digital version. The book title is set in Ex Ponto by Jovica Veljović.

Book design by Valerie Brewster, Scribe Typography. Printed on archival quality Glatfelter Author's Text at McNaughton & Gunn.